Utter ruin confronts the Earl of Tarrisbroke. Faced with discharging his father's mountainous gambling debts, he reluctantly agrees to trade his aristocratic title for a plebeian fortune. Marianne Johnson, the wealthy young widow of an elderly merchant, is furious to find herself chosen as a fortune-hunter's bride. But before the Earl can discover his widow's true worth, or Marianne realises that fortune-hunters can be devastatingly attractive, they have to unite to protect the priceless Crown of St Helen Theodora at Tarris-broke Hall....

By the same author in Masquerade

THE ABDUCTED HEIRESS

Tarrisbroke Hall
Jasmine Cresswell

MILLS & BOON LIMITED
London · Sydney · Toronto

*First published in Great Britain 1979 by
Robert Hale Limited, Clerkenwell House,
Clerkenwell Green, London EC1R 0HT*

© Jasmine Cresswell 1979

*This edition published 1980 by
Mills & Boon Limited, 15–16 Brook's Mews,
London W1Y 1LF*

*Australian copyright 1980
Philippine copyright 1980*

ISBN 0 263 73232 0

This book is sold subject to the condition that it shall not, by way of trade or otherwise, be lent, re-sold, hired out or otherwise circulated without the prior consent of Mills & Boon Limited in any form of binding or cover other than that in which it is published and without a similar condition including this condition being imposed on the subsequent purchaser.

The text of this publication or any part thereof may not be reproduced or transmitted in any form or by any means, electronic or mechanical, including photocopying, recording, storage in an information retrieval system, or otherwise, without the written permission of Robert Hale Limited.

*Printed and bound in Great Britain by
Cox and Wyman Ltd., Reading*

CHAPTER ONE

Sir Henry Lane surveyed the assembled company of guests with a jaundiced eye. After two months of junketing around Europe in the wake of the Bourbon court he was weary of the glittering parties, and had started to think longingly of London and the quiet orchards of his estate in Kent. A lifetime spent in the service of his Government had developed Sir Henry's natural strain of cynicism, but he found the fickle loyalties of his Italian hosts more than he could comfortably bear.

A slight stir of excitement attracted his attention, and glancing across to the marble staircase he saw that Viscount Rodbourne, his nephew, had finally decided to grace one of the *Contessa* Barbazone's parties with his much sought after presence. Sir Henry looked at the Viscount's pale face and noted with exasperation the lines of mingled strain and dissipation that had started to etch themselves on to his nephew's harsh features. He reflected ascerbically that the sooner the Viscount's father, otherwise known as the Right Honourable, the Earl of Tarrisbroke, succumbed to the combined effects of chronic alcoholism and a lifetime spent hunched up over the card tables, the better it would be for all concerned.

Sir Henry experienced a sudden, unexpected spurt of

sympathy for his nephew who, for the past ten years, had been forced to stand helplessly on the sidelines and watch as the Earl gambled away the fruits of a landed inheritance dating from the sixteenth century. It was little wonder, thought Sir Henry, that the Viscount had scarcely waited to attain his majority before sailing away from the frustrations of his native land and embarking upon a way of life made conspicuous chiefly by the beauty and dazzling variety of his mistresses.

Sir Henry decided to ignore for once the claims of several distinguished French Government officials, and made his way to the side of the ballroom, where Viscount Rodbourne could be seen dancing the quadrille with the woman widely reputed to be his current mistress. The *Principessa* Maria Gabriella, now busily conducting an expert flirtation with the Viscount, was the proud possessor of a comfortably wealthy husband, a cousin who was reigning Prince in the Italian province of Ancona, and a flawless olive skin that Napoleon Bonaparte himself had declared to be the most perfect complexion in Europe. She danced divinely, had an attractive smile and—other than a certain addiction to wearing large and elaborate pieces of jewellery all over her body—was invariably dressed in magnificent and tasteful fashion.

Tonight she shimmered in a gala robe of almost transparent gold tissue, her head and neck a blaze of multicoloured jewels. Viscount Rodbourne, with a sense of irony that was probably wasted on the *Principessa* but was much appreciated by his uncle, had chosen to clothe himself in unrelieved black. Only the white ruffles of his shirt stood out from the sombre velvet of his evening coat, and a single diamond glittered among the folds of his cravat.

The Viscount's absorption in the laughing conversation of his partner was not as great as it seemed, for at the conclusion of the set he escorted Maria Gabriella to the side of her next partner, and immediately crossed the ballroom floor to greet his uncle.

"Well, sir, this is an unexpected pleasure. I did not think that our Government allowed you to leave King Louis unattended. I have the impression that they fear he may return to chopping off the heads of Bourbon enemies if you are not there to restrain him."

Sir Henry Lane laughed wryly. "You over-estimate my influence with King Louis, my dear boy. It would take an army of British officials to prevent Louis' supporters indulging in a little bloodshed after so many years of exile."

He lowered his voice and remarked in tones of genuine bewilderment. "You know, sometimes I ask myself what would be required to convince the French monarchists that it is better to win a man's affection than to chop off his head. I'm afraid Louis is like all the other Bourbons—a slow learner."

The Viscount shrugged graceful shoulders. "I am sure Paris already regrets its eager adoption of the white lily. It would not take a very well organized group of revolutionaries to topple the Bourbons once again."

"My dear Quentin!" Sir Henry was horrified. "I beg you to exercise a little caution. You must watch what you say! As an Englishman, without any official position, your presence in Paris makes me constantly uneasy."

Viscount Rodbourne spoke lightly. "You should not trouble yourself, my dear sir. I have long ago decided that the devil is taking care of me for a special purpose of his own. I sometimes feel quite indestructible! Besides, Paris will soon be rid of me. Maria Gabriella informs me that she pines for the sight of her native land and wishes me to escort her into Italy." He added prosaically, "The truth of it is probably that her husband has summoned her back to Ancona and threatened to cut off her funds if she doesn't come." Once again his shoulders lifted in a delicate shrug. "But it makes no odds to me where I am located, so I will accompany her to Ancona if that gives her pleasure."

Sir Henry spoke abruptly, avoiding his nephew's gaze. "I have today received a letter from your mother." He waited hopefully, but upon receiving no comment from the Viscount, he reluctantly pressed on. "Your sister made her début this Season, and it seems likely that she will contract an eligible alliance with one of your neighbours."

The Viscount spoke curtly. "I am pleased, for my sister's sake." Then, almost against his will, he added, "I trust that my mother is well?"

"Yes," said Sir Henry. "She is as well as can be expected. But your father is sick, Quentin, and he is not expected to survive the month." He stole a glance at the marble-like rigidity of the Viscount's expression, and cleared his throat nervously. He was evidently experiencing an uncharacteristic difficulty in finding appropriate words. "I was wondering if you might care to make the journey across the Channel before it is too late," he said finally. "There cannot be many days of life left to your father."

The Viscount raised his quizzing glass and peered with exaggerated curiosity across the room. "My dear uncle, do look at what has arrived. Every time that I see the *Chevalier* de Veronne I believe that he will never again have the power to shock me, and every time I prove myself wrong! Would you but glance at that extraordinary waistcoat?"

Sir Henry tried once more. "Quentin. . . ."

Viscount Rodbourne turned to his uncle and spoke very gently. "I believe I must accompany the *Principessa*, my dear sir, as I had already planned. She has come to rely upon me in these small matters." He looked at his uncle's crestfallen features and allowed the mask to drop for a few moments. "Ah uncle! We have nothing to say to one another, my father and I. Believe me! It is not too late *now* —it was too late for us many years ago. I shall wait for Mr. Cowper to summon me to London, and then I shall return to England. My mother and sister will find me ready to do all in my power to make up for the long years of our estrangement. I desire nothing more than to settle down in England with an amiable wife of meek disposition. Now, my dear sir, I think I must beg you to leave this subject quite . . . in fact, absolutely . . . alone."

Sir Henry acknowledged defeat. "Do not leave Paris without informing me of your direction, Quentin. You will no doubt wish me to pass on any messages which may arrive for you from the lawyer."

Viscount Rodbourne opened his snuff-box with an elegant flick of one wrist, offering it to Sir Henry. "I am, as ever, in your debt. And now I see our hostess bearing down upon us in a fashion that precludes the possibility of escape. Only let us hope that she has not found some new Bourbon princess for me to dance with. My toes have not yet recovered from an experience last week with a lady of regrettably abundant charms."

Sir Henry spoke in a moment of unguarded irritation. "Dammit, Quentin, you are capable of doing something better with your time than squiring dubious Royals around the fringes of European society."

Viscount Rodbourne smiled. "Come now, uncle. Would you describe my role in precisely those terms? I had rather prided myself on the fact that I have been able to help you on several occasions. There are not many Englishmen, you know, who have the entrée into virtually every court in Europe."

Sir Henry spoke shrewdly. "You may count yourself lucky that our hostess has almost achieved her passage across the ballroom floor, and I am thus prevented from speaking frankly. We both know that while you consider the doors of London society closed to you, your success in Europe is little more than salt rubbed into a wound."

The Viscount greeted his hostess with a low bow, that successfully masked his expression. "*Signora Contessa*, you have arrived in the nick of time. I was on the point of asking my uncle how he has avoided death at the hands of his irate colleagues for so many years. His ruthless exposure of all the weak parts in my character was becoming painful."

The Contessa tapped Sir Henry's arm with her fan. "Then you shall come with me, Sir Henry, and meet a strange man from the Americas, who is dressed all in brown and wears woollen stockings." She smiled archly at the Viscount. "Dear sir, I cannot have my two most interesting Englishmen at odds with one another. Look! I see that the *Principessa* Maria Gabriella is coming to speak with you, and I think we shall leave her to nurse you back into a good humour with all the world."

Viscount Rodbourne raised plump fingers to his lips and avoided his uncle's searching eyes. "At one of your parties, *Signora Contessa*, it is impossible to feel anything but good-humoured."

Maria Gabriella disposed herself upon a day couch in her dressing room, and allowed the diaphanous gauze of her *robe de chambre* to float seductively open from the baby blue ribbons tied at her throat. She lay back against the cushions, comfortably aware that her soft, rounded body was now displayed to its best advantage. Viscount Rodbourne wound a fresh cravat carelessly round his neck, tucking the ends into a creditable *trone d'amour* without visible effort. His mind was full of the family news given him that evening by Sir Henry, and he was finding Maria Gabriella's opulent charms a somewhat unwelcome distraction. He looked dispassionately at her voluptuous body, the seductive tangle of dark hair flowing over her shoulders, and he was conscious of a slight frisson of distaste. He tried to crush the thought, remembering the passion that this same body had aroused in him less than an hour before. He walked quickly to the *Principessa's* side, dropped down on to the sofa and rested his arm gently on her body, hastily snatching her fingers and dropping a kiss on each one when she moved to run her hands through the springy strands of his hair.

"Ah no!" he laughed. "Even for you, *carissima*, I cannot allow my cravat to be disarranged. And I have to leave you now if we are to set off for the Adriatic tomorrow. There are tasks that I must put in hand. My servant must be given his instructions, and the landlord informed of my intention to depart."

Maria Gabriella pouted. "Always you English wish to be so organized. I have a much bigger house here than you, but I do not plan to waste the night in preparation for tomorrow. There are better things to do." She leaned towards him as she spoke, allowing her gown to fall open, so that her soft, white body pressed against the muslin of the Viscount's shirt.

With infinite tact he extricated himself from her embrace, and continued the seemingly languid pace of his dressing. "Nevertheless, *cara*, I feel that I cannot emulate your excellent lack of preparation. We English are afflicted with the most rigid of childhood educations, and become martyrs to the systems imposed upon us in the nursery. Do not disturb my equilibrium by attempting to shatter my established routine, I beg of you."

With the total inconsequence which the Viscount had long since learned to tolerate, the *Principessa* changed the subject. "My brother is angry with me. He does not like that I shall be involved with you in so many celebrations for King Louis. He does not have faith that King Louis will remain the king. What do you think, Quentin?"

The Viscount looked at Maria Gabriella with a sudden flash of concern. "I think, *cara*, that your brother should take care in showing his dislike of King Louis. It is known to the British Government that he was an ardent supporter of Bonaparte's government, and this is not a moment to wave such views like a banner. Rather than reproaching you, the *Conte* di Mazaretto should attempt to consolidate his position with your cousin, the Prince, and with the British troops stationed in the Province." He searched the perfect regularity of her features, hoping to discover some trace of emotion or understanding in her eyes, but she had been trained from childhood to believe that a doll-like and empty prettiness constituted the epitome of female beauty, and so now, as always, her face remained a blank. Her lips eventually formed a delicate pout, and impatiently the Viscount asked, "Is this why you wish to return to Ancona? Your brother has ordered you there?"

The pout became slightly more pronounced, and for a moment he thought she might be about to reveal the true reasons for her sudden urgent desire to remove from Paris. But, with the instinctive secretiveness that she had long since learned was her best measure of self-protection, she turned aside his question with a trill of laughter. "Oh la, Quentin! You are becoming too curious. I have told you that I wish to return to Ancona because I need to see the sun. Paris is a dull city—all grey skies and rain. We Italians need sunshine or we start to wither."

The Viscount accepted her mood. He felt a certain sense of protective obligation towards the *Principessa*, chiefly because he distrusted the volatile political manœuvrings of her brother and her husband. But his deeper feelings remained untouched by her, and—he admitted it almost with reluctance—the burning attraction he had once felt towards her body was beginning to pall.

Nevertheless, he summoned up a smile to match her own and murmured gallantly, "You need no sunshine, *carissima*. I have found your beauty blossoming under the autumn rains."

She sighed contentedly and moved into his arms. "Ah,

Quentin! In your compliments, you are not an Englishman. Sometimes, when you make love to me it is as if you were indeed a native of our beautiful, warm country. Soon, *caro mio*, you will forget that you were born in such a cold and ugly island, and think you have always belonged to Italy."

She felt him stiffen in her arms, and he moved sharply away from her. "You are mistaken, Maria Gabriella, if you think that my native land is forgotten." He sighed at the impossibility of confiding any of his deeper emotions and struggles to this woman, or to any of the women who had graced his bed over the past years of voluntary exile. In the end, he decided regretfully, when the hours of lovemaking were finished, there was little point of contact between a man and a woman.

He knew that she could not begin to understand such thoughts, so he touched her softly on the cheek. "I must go now, Maria Gabriella. I shall see you here tomorrow morning, and I will take you back to Ancona." He raised her hand and kissed the soft palm. "I may have to go back to England soon, even though you consider it a cold and ugly island. It will be better if you are safely returned to your native city, with many members of your family ready to protect you."

Maria Gabriella sighed discontentedly. "They know how to protect me—yes, that is true. But you, Quentin, you know how to love me. What shall I do if you are far away from me, locked in your so freezing castle, full of gloomy servants?"

The Viscount looked at her sardonically, and gently kissed the tips of her fingers. "I should suggest, dear Maria Gabriella, that you find another lover." And with these words, he closed the door of her bedroom leaving the *Principessa* wondering, not for the first time, whether she actually exercised any control over the Viscount's emotions whatsoever.

CHAPTER TWO

The lawyer polished his eye-glasses with a large silk handkerchief, rubbing at an invisible particle of dust with grim concentration. With evident reluctance he finally perched the spectacles on the end of his nose, and shuffled the impressive pile of documents that littered his desk.

The former Viscount Rodbourne, now fifth Earl of Tarrisbroke, eyed him cynically. "You may stop procrastinating, Cowper, and tell me the worst. I have long been reconciled to the idea that my late, unlamented father would reduce us all to penury."

The lawyer removed his spectacles and examined them hopefully, but no smear or speck of dust offered an excuse for further delay. He cleared his throat. "You say, my lord, that you have long been inured to the thought of penury. I do not think, however, that you can be aware of the extent to which the late Earl had . . . er . . . speculated."

The Earl laughed without noticeable mirth. "My imagination is pretty vivid, Cowper, and I have plenty of past experience to help round out the picture. You, even if nobody else, must know that my prolonged residence abroad was a direct consequence of my father's activities at the gaming tables. Not to mention his frequently expressed dislike of my presence at Tarrisbroke."

"What precisely do you mean, my lord?"

"Heavens above, Cowper! Surely you are aware of the conversation I had with my father on the day I attained my majority? My . . . revered . . . parent greeted me with the news that the lands normally bestowed on the heir to the earldom had been sold to meet his gambling debts. Debts of honour, I believe he termed them! It was then that I decided life might prove less expensive to sustain on the Continent. An income of six hundred pounds a year does not allow one the freedom of choice that one might wish, you know." He smiled without rancour. "However, I should not complain. The activities of *Monsieur* Bonaparte have made my years abroad . . . interesting . . . to say the least."

Mr. Cowper appeared anything but reassured by this new information, and calming himself by drawing several deep breaths he finally burst into speech. "I knew nothing of the conversation you mention, my lord. Indeed for the past several years I have laboured under the misapprehension that the income from the Norfolk estates was yours to enjoy." His shoulders hunched in an agitated heap behind the piles of paper. "I ask you to forgive my disorganized presentation of the facts to your lordship. The truth of the matter is that the case seems so desperate that I hardly know where to begin. The Norfolk estates represented my last hope. I had counted on finding them maintained in good order."

"Cowper, I feel you have now suitably prepared me for the depressing nature of your tidings. For God's sake, man, proceed with the actual details. I beg you to remember that I have been travelling for ten days across Europe and

I can think of nothing save hot water, a shave and the comforts of a bed. All other matters are beginning to seem of little moment."

The lawyer drew towards him a deep leather box, and reluctantly unwound several papers tied neatly with red ribbons. "It has to be admitted that the late Earl did not always manage his affairs in the way I might have wished." With sad dignity, Mr. Cowper turned to face the new Earl. "I attempted to remonstrate with your father on numerous occasions, my lord. Indeed, while always mindful of the different stations in life to which we had been called, I would make bold to suggest that I remonstrated with him quite severely, but to no avail. In fact, I fear that I have done you nought but a disservice, for on the death of your father it became apparent that many transactions had occurred which had been deliberately concealed from me." Mournfully he tapped some papers. "I hold here, for example, what I thought to be the deeds to your personal estates in Norfolk. They must obviously be mere duplicates, since you have just told me that the land passed out of your possession more than ten years ago."

The Earl stood up from the comfortable chair where he had been lounging and walked across the faded expanse of Turkish carpet to the small window. He looked out on to the narrow street only for a moment, before turning to confront the lawyer.

"All right. I see that this is not a moment for frivolity. In round terms, I suppose you are telling me that there is little ready cash, and that the estates are in even more disastrous order than they were when I left England. Is that about the size of it?"

Mr. Cowper hesitated, then spoke in a rush of unexpected firmness. "There is *no* ready cash, my lord. Everything which might be sold has been sold. Your grandfather's fine stable of horses, for example, was auctioned off almost eight years ago. The paintings from Rodbourne House have all gone. Tarrisbroke Hall itself is urgently in need of refurbishing."

The Earl laughed without much humour. "It is obviously fortunate that an income of six hundred pounds a year has already instilled in me some notions of economy. Had I been looking to my inheritance to salvage me from debt, I should certainly have been looking in vain." He smiled through tight lips. "Take heart, Cowper. My boyish desires for adventure disappeared when Bonaparte annexed the province of Ancona for the second time. Fleeing through Europe in a peasant's cart may be considered an adventure the first time it occurs. On the second occasion it has to be accounted a dead bore. I now desire nothing more than to settle down and become a farmer. I shall retire to the country and study Mr. Arthur Young's new ideas about growing turnips. I shall only emerge into the light of town when my sister needs to refurbish her wardrobe. I do not say that all will be righted by next summer, but in five years we may hope that the land is beginning to come about."

The lawyer continued to shuffle his papers, and avoided meeting the Earl's eye. "My lord, you have not heard it all. Certainly you are right in suggesting that the estates *could* be made to turn a comfortable profit. In your grandfather's day, Tarrisbroke lands produced an income far in excess of ten thousand pounds a year, and there is no reason why they should not be made to generate such sums again."

"Then we are in agreement," the Earl interrupted impatiently. "Cowper, my man, I do thank you for your concern. And I shall return to you tomorrow so that I can ask for your excellent advice on every matter that currently presses for attention. But just now I am truly exhausted, and I must leave you for this evening. Only tell me how many days I should plan to stay on in town. Come, Cowper. Do you need me for three days? A week? A sennight?"

Cowper dropped his eyes to the desk and spoke very fast.

"The land is mortgaged, my lord. The payments are seriously in arrears. Tarrisbroke Hall itself and the Home Farm have illegally been pledged twice. Your creditors could have taken possession of the Hall in your absence, but as a courtesy to you—and at my earnest entreaty—they have waited for your return. You are ruined, my lord. Utterly ruined."

The blood drained from the Earl's face, exposing the lines of fatigue and the grey pallor of exhaustion that marked his cheeks. "I see," he said, returning to his seat by the fire. "It was foolish of me to place any reliance whatsoever upon my father's sense of obligation to his family and his heritage. I have certainly had ample evidence in the past that the claims of duty made no impression on him when he found himself in front of a card table."

Mr. Cowper coughed apologetically. "Unfortunately, my lord, it must be admitted that the attraction of the late Earl to all forms of gambling was notorious. So unlike your grandfather and, I think, unlike yourself."

The Earl shrugged his shoulders. "When I wish for excitement, I find there are more diverting ways of obtaining it than staking coins on the turn of a card." He turned his face into the shadows. "It is . . . painful . . . for me to think that Tarrisbroke Hall will pass out of our family, but since I do not possess the resources to redeem my father's pledges, I can only ask for your assistance in carrying out the practical necessities connected with its sale."

The lawyer inclined his head. "You know that I shall always be honoured to be of service to the Earls of Tarrisbroke."

The Earl spoke dryly. "Considering the way they have undoubtedly treated you, that is most generous. I only wish your wise counsel had been allowed to prevail." He stopped himself abruptly. "However, it is useless to repine. We must see what arrangements can be made for the removal of the Dowager Countess and my sister to town. It will be best, I think, if they spend a few weeks with me in London before we attempt to re-organize their permanent living arrangements. Fortunately, my mother's jointure, though not large, is more than adequate to support her in a house of moderate size."

The lawyer passed an agitated hand across his eyes. "My lord, even now you have not heard the extent of the financial disaster threatening your family. In a document drawn up by another lawyer, your father has assigned the income from your mother's lands to one of his creditors. The land, thank God, was secure from sale by him and will eventually revert to your sister. Lady Eleanor's portion is, therefore, safe. The Dowager Countess, however, is totally without means of support."

The Earl sprang to his feet, the chair crashing unheeded

to the ground as he flung it away from him. "This is too much! Why was I not informed of the disastrous route my father was taking? All else I could have tolerated, but it is insupportable that my mother and sister should be left in financial straits that are beyond my power to rectify." Angrily he strode up and down the room. "It is my own fault," he said at last. "I should not have allowed false pride to come between me and my responsibility to the members of my family. I could not bear to watch my father's excesses and now, because of some foolish youthful notions of honour, I have to contemplate the Dowager Countess begging for support from whichever member of her family may choose to be generous. My father must have been mad!"

Mr. Cowper observed his client's outburst with silent sympathy, but he could not smother the hopeful gleam that crept into his expression. Long years in practice as a legal adviser to the aristocracy had developed both his innate tact and his inborn sense of timing. If ever the Earl could be brought to agree to Mr. Cowper's plans, it would be now.

The lawyer walked round from his desk, quietly righted the position of the fallen chair, and poured two glasses of his best brandy, watching the Earl as he tossed back the liquor at a single gulp, thrusting the glass out for a second serving. Mr. Cowper refilled the glass, still without speaking, and once the brandy had been consumed, the Earl turned to his lawyer with a small grimace. "Forgive my display of rudeness, Cowper. Your revelations came as a very great shock to me."

"As they did to me, my lord. I could not have expected

you to take such news calmly. May I ask what you plan to do now?"

The Earl shrugged. "What can I do? I shall endeavour to establish my mother and sister in a small house—perhaps in Bath—and trust that my sister makes an early marriage. As the daughter of an earl, and with a modest competence of her own, we can hope for a reasonable match."

"And what of yourself, my lord?"

"I confess to being a little weary of travel, but it seems that I have no choice other than to appeal to my uncle, who has just recently been called back from France and asked to lead our Government's embassy to the Emperor of all the Russias. I trust that he may find employment for me on his staff. I am too old for a soldier and not suited for a career in the Church, so it seems I must become a diplomat. My former position as an adviser at the Court of Prince Alberto has left me with some first-hand experience of European politics, and I have been of assistance to my uncle on several occasions in the past."

He spoke dryly. "I realized several years since that my education, while ideally suited to the owner of a large estate, is sadly lacking in the skills needed for the serious pursuit of a profession. Schoolboy Greek and an intimate knowledge of the ways of the Polite World will hardly open many doors to a man."

Mr. Cowper looked at him shrewdly. "I think you would prefer to remain upon your estate in England, my lord."

The Earl responded impatiently. "I have already said that I am weary of travelling. But in this instance there is little difficulty in deciding to return to the Continent. There is, I believe, some saying to the effect that beggars cannot be choosers."

"In this instance, my lord, I believe there is an alternative open to you, although I do not expect you to find the choice an attractive one."

"It is marvellous to discover that I have any options to consider. Pray enlighten me."

Mr. Cowper examined the cuff of his black serge coat. "You could marry, my lord."

For a moment the Earl looked at the lawyer in stupefied silence, and then a great burst of laughter filled the darkening office. "If I did not know you better, Cowper, I should swear that you were jesting. Leaving aside the fact that I am no longer acquainted with any of the young ladies currently on offer by doting Society matrons, just how do you suggest that I phrase my proposals? Should I mention first the utter lack of financial resources? Or should I perhaps stress the need for an immediate wedding so that we may enjoy our honeymoon with a roof still over our heads? On the other hand, perhaps I should resist the temptation to mention such sordid details and merely stress the depth of my passion? Surely that would be no more ridiculous than anything else about taking a wife at this point in my life?"

"If you have quite finished, my lord, I shall be able to explain to you what I have in mind."

"My God, Cowper, I do believe you are serious!"

"Never more so in my life, my lord."

The Earl spoke stiffly. "Marriage is not a state that holds out great attractions to me at the best of times. I do not find the thought of a permanent female companion pleasant. It is hard to see, in my present circumstances, how I could tolerate the added burdens a wife would impose."

"The wife I have in mind, my lord, would remove many of the burdens that surround you at present."

"You are no doubt suggesting a union with some Divine Being, for I fail to see how a mere mortal—especially a female—could find a solution to the problems I now face."

"I do not suggest an angel, my lord. Merely an extremely rich widow."

The Earl rose to his feet and from the advantage of rather more than six feet, looked down with deceptive mildness at the five feet four inches of Mr. Cowper. "Ah!" he said meditatively. "An extremely rich widow. I gather that you have a specific ... lady ... in mind."

"Yes, my lord. I have met the lady and understand she would be willing to consider such a match."

"I wonder what particular deformities I am supposed to overlook in this delightfully willing bride? If her dowry is sufficient to take care of *my* financial burdens, then she must have a truly disastrous defect to overcome. A hunchback perhaps? Or else she is entirely lame? It cannot be mere lack of beauty, for a large enough fortune will persuade any number of men to forgive mere plainness of features."

"Mrs. Johnson is not plain, my lord. Indeed, other than a slightly greater height than some men might find appealing, I think it would be fair to say that Mrs. Johnson is something of a beauty. It is not her looks any more than her fortune which is at fault, my lord." He paused for a moment, then spoke bluntly. "It is her birth. Her father was a tradesman, and so was her late husband. Her brother has manufacturies in the north of England."

The Earl flicked a speck of dust from the sleeve of his coat and responded with exaggerated formality. "It is good of you to make this suggestion to me, Cowper. I know you have always my best interests at heart. However, I do not think that I have yet sunk so low that I must maintain the outward dignities of our family at the expense of my personal integrity." He reached into a waistcoat pocket and examined the timepiece he carried there. "I see that it is way past your dinner-time, Cowper. I must not detain you further."

"You go too fast, my lord. I think it would be better if you did not dismiss this suggestion quite so hastily."

The Earl spoke curtly. "I see that I must remind you, Cowper, that *I* am not a tradesman. I do not consider myself a saleable commodity."

"Noble sentiments, my lord," said the lawyer with deceptive mildness. "You prefer, perhaps, that the Dowager Countess should be considered a beggar?"

"Damn it, Cowper, I cannot accept such statements from you!"

"The truth, my lord, is frequently unpleasant. It nevertheless remains the truth."

Wearily the Earl sank back into the chair. "Perhaps you are right. Who am I to prate of the family honour after all that you have been forced to tell me this evening? Tell me about your Mrs. Johnson, Cowper. Is she old? Is there any hope that I could marry her and soon be a widower? What of her behaviour? Is it . . . unbearably . . . vulgar?"

"I have met Mrs. Johnson only on one occasion, my lord. Her brother is better known to me since we have had frequent dealings in regard to the mortgages on the Tarrisbroke estates. Mr. Perkins—that is the name of Mrs. Johnson's brother—holds the first mortgage on Tarrisbroke Hall."

"I see. And what is your impression of Mr. Perkins and his sister?"

"Mr. Perkins is a tradesman, my lord. He does not pretend to be otherwise. He is a shrewd merchant and a successful manufacturer. I have found him always to be honest and forthright. It was he who suggested the possibility of this match to me when the full extent of your financial problems became apparent. He makes no bones about the fact that he has been on the lookout for an aristocrat to wed his sister ever since her first husband died. Mrs. Johnson was in India with her husband, I believe, and she survived the journey home but he did not."

"She is no doubt brown and wizened by the sun, in addition to being bred up in a commercial spirit?"

"As to that, my lord, she is certainly dark, but I do not recall that her skin was particularly wrinkled. I spoke to her only briefly—I was introduced when I was a guest at her brother's house, you understand—but she seems a modest, unassuming young woman. Quiet and deferential in her brother's presence, as is only proper of course. But dignified in her speech, my lord. I understand she was educated at Miss Beale's Seminary for Young Ladies, which as you know, is the very best. Her godfather is Sir William Kenneth, and I believe he repaid some financial obligation to Mrs. Johnson's father by sponsoring her admission to Miss Beale's. So you will find she has every refinement. Plays the pianoforte, sings and writes poetry. Everything you could wish for."

"Indeed," said the Earl sarcastically. "With such accomplishments what more could any prospective groom demand?"

Mr. Cowper was relieved to see that his client appeared to be accepting his fate with proper resignation. Tentatively he ventured a question. "Do I have your permission to tell Mr. Perkins that you are prepared to continue the negotiations, my lord? Some preliminary financial arrangements have already been agreed upon—subject to your approval of course." He hurried on, before the Earl could break into speech. "Would you, perhaps, care to meet the lady in question?"

"It would probably be better if I saved that treat for my wedding day, since I clearly have no choice in the matter." Angrily he swept his hand across the lawyer's desk, scattering papers in random heaps over the floor. "Oh, there's no need to look like that, Cowper. I'll see her and say all that is pretty. God knows we had better furbish up the sale as best we can. Perhaps we can even persuade the Dowager Countess that it is a love match!"

Cowper ignored the sarcasm and nodded approvingly. "That would be a very wise decision, my lord. Now you are behaving sensibly, just as I knew you would. Mrs. Johnson has travelled extensively for one so young, particularly in view of the highly unsettled state of the Continent over the past few years. We could probably give out the information that you and Mrs. Johnson met abroad."

The Earl laughed bitterly. "I know I can rely upon you, Cowper, to put the best possible gloss on this miserable affair. Let us hope that Mrs. Johnson considers the title of Countess and a decrepit mansion in the country fair exchange for so many thousands of her pounds sterling."

"She will be acquiring a very desirable husband, my lord. There are many ladies who will envy her good fortune."

The Earl spoke softly. "Mrs. Johnson's money will be buying my estates, my houses, my horses, my family name and a measure of my protection. I wish you to make it quite plain to her, however, that she will *not* be acquiring me. Her funds—magnificent as they may be—are insufficient for such a purchase."

The lawyer replied soothingly. "Never fear, my lord. I shall see to it that your wishes are carried out in every detail. Mr. Perkins is a shrewd man of affairs and he will be happy to accommodate your needs. Mrs. Johnson, although a widow, is not yet twenty-two. You will probably find her quite unused to forming her own opinion and quite willing to do whatever you desire."

"Enough, Cowper. I have heard enough for today. Come round to Rodbourne House tomorrow and tell me what arrangements you have made for my meeting with this wonderfully docile widow. I wish to have everything settled before I leave for the country and a reunion with the members of my family."

CHAPTER THREE

"I will not do it! I refuse! You cannot make me!"

Thomas Perkins shifted uneasily in his armchair and looked warily at the stormy expression of his sister. "Now, now, Marianne," he said experimentally. "You know very well that you would like to be a countess. Any woman would."

"Well, I am not *any* woman. I am me, and I do not wish to marry some grouchy old Earl who has run through his fortune and has decided to forgive me the smell of the shop so long as I come perfumed with enough money bags!"

Mr. Perkins winced. He was frequently forced to the conclusion that his father's good brass had been sadly wasted at Miss Beale's Select Seminary for Young Ladies. "Marianne," he murmured reprovingly. "That isn't the way your Father would have wanted to hear you talk." He rushed into further speech before his sister could find time to interject another indelicate comment. "Besides, the Earl of Tarrisbroke is not old. He is a young man of two-and-thirty. And a fine looking fellow so Mr. Cowper tells me."

"Mr. Cowper?" Marianne whirled round to confront her brother. "You mean the lawyer whom I met at luncheon here last week is the Earl of Tarrisbroke's lawyer?" She laughed scornfully. "No wonder you did not dare to tell me what his business was."

"Now come along, lass. You can't stay a widow all your life. You're a young woman, and one day you'll be wanting to have children of your own. You have to marry somebody. Why not this Earl?"

Marianne's expression softened slightly as she looked at the earnest appeal in her brother's face. "I have already been married once to a man of your choosing, Thomas, and I have no wish to repeat the experiment."

"Horace Johnson was a good man," said Thomas Perkins indignantly. "He and our father did business together for years, and Horace never put a foot wrong. Wonderful business head he had, and as kind as the day is long."

Marianne sighed. "You are quite right, Thomas. Horace was indeed kind and I have no doubt that his business acumen was truly remarkable. I fear, though, that I am regrettably hard to satisfy where husbands are concerned. I require other qualities than kindness and sound financial sense. There must be some interests in common, some spark of fellow feeling. Perhaps I am even romantic enough to hope there could be love."

Thomas Perkins seized on the part of the speech he found easiest to understand. "Well, what could be more romantic than marrying an earl?" he asked reasonably. "Most girls in your situation would be carrying on something remarkable at the thought of becoming a real live countess. After all, you can't expect to find anybody very romantic when you're living with me next door to the manufactury. And you can't stay in London on your own, my girl, and that's flat."

"Miss Thatcher did say that she would be pleased to stay

and keep me company, Thomas. Surely she is now old enough to be accounted a suitable chaperone? After all, I have been married!"

"No!" Thomas closed his snuffbox with a decided snap. "You are too young. I am your guardian until you are twenty-five, and I'm telling you to marry the Earl. Sometimes a man has to be firm in taking his decisions. I can't let myself be influenced by your opinions, Marianne. You're still nought but a chit of a lass when all's said and done, and I can't expect you to know which side your bread is buttered."

"Why are you so certain that I shall be better cared for if I am married? I have scarcely finished my year of mourning for Horace and now, when I have my first chance of freedom, you tell me that I must sacrifice my independence yet again. What is so marvellous about wedding an earl?"

"Really, Marianne, sometimes you shock me. If you can't see the advantages of being wed to a peer of the realm, then I don't see how I am going to explain them to you. I know *I* shall be mighty proud to talk about my sister the countess, and that's a fact!"

"No doubt it will be marvellous for trade," said Marianne bitterly.

"Not a doubt of it," said Thomas cheerfully ignoring his sister's sarcasm. "Cowper tells me he is bringing the Earl round here before Evening Service on Sunday. So you make sure you're looking your best my girl. None of those dowdy old greys and lavenders you've been wearing recently."

"No, if you say not, Thomas." A sudden flash of animation crossed Marianne's features, although it was quickly suppressed. "Would it be too late to have the carriage brought round, dear Thomas? I have just decided that I will ask the *modiste* to fashion me a new dress in which to receive his lordship. You are right that I have allowed myself to become too drab just lately."

Thomas smiled benignly at his sister. Ladies and new dresses fitted well together in his scheme of things, and since he was an affectionate brother, it always relieved him when Marianne consented to behave like the other females of his acquaintance. "I'm sure it's never too late in the afternoon to indulge a lady in a little shopping spree." He patted Marianne lovingly on the arm. "Now you run upstairs and fetch Miss Thatcher and your bonnet, and I'll see about the carriage. Make sure you order something eye-catching for the Earl! We want to surprise him."

Marianne smiled mistily at her brother. "That's *exactly* what I had in mind, Thomas," she murmured. "How splendid it is when we see eye-to-eye in this manner."

"You're a smart looking lass, Marianne, I'll say that for you. Nobody would ever know you'd spent two years out among all those savages, burning up under that heathen sunshine. You tell Madame Yvonne, or whatever she calls herself, that she can send her bill to me. It'll be a pleasure to see you looking your best."

"You are too good to me sometimes, Thomas." Marianne turned away abruptly. "Are you *sure* you could not reconsider these wedding plans?"

"Now, now, Marianne. I thought that was all settled. You worry your pretty little head about the dress, and I shall see to it that the Earl knows that he has to treat you right. I'll see that it's written in to the marriage contract that you have a large allowance to spend just as you wish. You'll be able to have a bit of fun at last. I daresay you'll hardly see the Earl after the first few months, anyway. I understand these aristocrats never spend more than a few weeks of each year together."

"A true union of the spirit," said Marianne ironically, and then seeing that her brother was looking puzzled again she turned and kissed him lightly on the cheek, feeling full of contrition. "I am out of humour today, Thomas. I shall go and buy a new dress and see if that may not serve to restore my good spirits."

"That's my girl. A new dress will turn the trick for a female every time."

"In this instance, Thomas, I am hoping fervently that you are right."

Thomas Perkins nodded happily. His sister was a good girl most of the time, and if she could ever grow out of the childish habit of thinking her own opinion every bit as important as that of the menfolk around her, she would make some man a wonderful wife.

As soon as he had rung for the carriage, his thoughts switched back to the tangled state of the Tarrisbroke finances. He had Cowper's word for it that the present Earl was a very different man from his father. Nevertheless, Thomas Perkins had not reached his present comfortable position by relying on other people's judgments. He would meet the Earl for himself, and if he looked all right he'd see that the marriage papers were drawn up so that none of the money settled on his little sister would ever find its way into profligate Tarrisbroke pockets. The hard-earned brass of Horace Johnson and Thomas Perkins Senior was never going to be tossed away on the gaming tables, he'd see to that!

Thomas helped himself to a generous pinch of snuff, wheezed contentedly, and settled down more snuggly against the cushions padding his wooden chair. Little Marianne about to be a countess! Mrs. Martha Perkins would gain such a commanding lead in social prestige over all the other Manchester ladies that there would be no catching her. They were good folk, his wife and his sister. Fine looking women both of them, although Marianne was a bit thin for his taste. Thomas Perkins' head nodded contentedly on to his chest, and he slept.

It was almost closing time when Marianne entered the elegant establishment presided over by Madame Yvonne de Blanchard, a lady of fashionably foreign appearance and fierce temper, who had been born in the heart of London's Spitalfields, and had never been closer to France than a week's excursion by stage-coach to the coastal port of Folkestone.

Marianne, who spoke alarmingly good French in comparison with most of her gently-nurtured contemporaries, always tactfully refrained from uttering a single phrase that was not in plain English when in Madame Yvonne's presence. Either because of this, or perhaps because of her trim figure and naturally chic taste, she invariably received excellent service from the *modiste*.

On Thursday afternoon, however, Madame Yvonne was hard put to maintain her smiling façade. She viewed Mrs. Johnson purchases with an increasing disfavour that rapidly sank into outright and incredulous condemnation.

Mrs. Johnson's choice of material for her new outfit left Madame Yvonne gasping for words, but her description of the style in which the material was to be cut, and the trim which she felt appropriate, caused Madame Yvonne's normally rigid control to desert her.

"Mrs. Johnson!" she exclaimed. "You ain't never goin' to do that!" Hastily she recollected herself, although the satin stripes of virulent purple and acid lilac were almost sufficient to overset her once again. She tried a more moderate protest. "If Madame chooses striped satin and then decides to decorate the gown with white lace *and* large velvet bows, I fear the results will be less elegant than Madame would wish. When I trained in Paris, the designer told me *never* to trim purple stripes with black velvet. It is of all things the most vulgar." Madame de Blanchard uttered the lies without a blink. After so many years of deception she had almost forgotten that her only training had occurred in a back room in London's East End rather than at a salon in Paris.

Marianne spoke reassuringly, avoiding her companion's eyes in so far as this was possible. "It is quite all right, Madame de Blanchard. I wish to purchase this particular outfit for a . . . for a little joke. I am aware of the fact that the finished result will be—er—rather startling."

Miss Thatcher was beginning to look agitated, and Madame de Blanchard slightly disappointed. Another of the pleasant things about serving Mrs. Johnson had always been her aura of calm good sense. It was distressing to find that she, no less than Madame's more aristocratic clients, was given to wild flights of fancy. Mentally Madame de Blanchard shrugged. Mrs. Johnson would undoubtedly pay promptly for the hideous creation that she was ordering, and this in itself was a blessing not to be lightly thrown away. The *modiste* swallowed all further comments, therefore, and promised delivery of the gown by Saturday evening. Marianne smiled in her usual friendly fashion, and bade the outraged dressmaker a tactfully swift good evening.

Miss Thatcher could hardly manage to contain her indignation until they were in the carriage. The barouche door had only just been closed when she burst into speech. "Now, Marianne, you may as well tell me what this expedition was all about. You can't hoax me into believing that you wish to purchase that horrendous gown just for a little joke. Pray tell me what disastrous scheme you have in mind now?"

"It's not a disastrous scheme, Helen. I hope it is a scheme to rescue me from disaster."

"Two years of Indian sunshine have undoubtedly addled my wits. Could you explain to me why purple and lilac stripes, not to mention lavender lace mittens and foaming white lace fichus, are likely to save you from disaster?"

Marianne sighed wearily. "Thomas wishes me to marry again." She saw Miss Thatcher's startled expression and said ruefully, "I was sure *you* had not been told of his plans!" Impatiently she pulled at the strings of her reticule. "Oh Helen! He has already selected my new husband for me, and I positively dread the thought of our first meeting. Mr. Johnson was a kind-hearted man, even if he was old enough to be my father. This time, Thomas is planning to marry me to some wretched earl who has already run through his own fortune and presumably now wishes to have the pleasure of running through mine. How can I agree to such a match, when I have longed so much for a taste of independence?"

Miss Thatcher thought silently and rapidly. As a single lady who had been forced by economic circumstance to earn her own living from the age of seventeen, she saw pleasures in the state of matrimony that escaped Marianne's more jaundiced eye. "Well, Marianne," she ventured cautiously. "There would undoubtedly be advantages in becoming a countess. And you know your brother is too shrewd to allow anybody the opportunity of running through your fortune. I'm sure the marriage settlements would offer you every protection." She looked at Marianne's stormy face and added a little apologetically, "You know, I have often thought that your talents and your education are being sadly wasted just at present. As the wife of an Earl you would have great opportunities to put your talents to good use."

"It is the Earl of Tarrisbroke who has been chosen as my bridegroom," said Marianne dryly. "To the best of my knowledge, the late earl spent a fortune at the gaming tables of London, and the present earl has spent the last ten years escorting the beauties of Europe from Court ballroom to ballroom. I cannot see that he would take much interest in my education, or in the useful employment of my domestic skills."

Miss Thatcher was visibly disconcerted. "The Earl of Tarrisbroke! Oh dear. . . ." Being unable to think of anything more positive to say concerning one of England's most notorious rakes, she turned the conversation. "I'm afraid I still don't understand the reason for those dreadful purple stripes."

Marianne looked confused. "Oh Helen! Even if I explain you will probably say they are just another one of my mad schemes. But you see, I wanted to buy an outfit that was startlingly vulgar, the sort of thing no lady would ever dream of wearing. The Earl's family has probably prided itself upon the unsullied purity of its lineage for ten generations, and I'm sure that whatever his financial straits my fortune cannot make the match altogether palatable to the Earl. I'm certain that he must fear that I am a wretchedly vulgar and grasping widow, who longs to climb the social heights by clinging to his coattails. That dreadful outfit is merely designed to confirm his worst fears." She looked earnestly at Helen, seeking some sympathy in her companion's face. "Don't you see? If he is hesitating on the brink of offering matrimony, if he is wondering whether or not to take the plunge and ally himself with the daughter of a shop-keeper, then I want to make sure that his worst nightmares are realised. My brother will not allow *me* to cry off from the match, so I shall try and persuade the Earl to cry off instead."

Miss Thatcher made a small sound of distress. "Oh Marianne! Are you so certain that life as a countess would not be more to your satisfaction than the life you lead now? Forgive me for speaking so bluntly, but it is impossible for me to believe that you find your present situation *entirely* happy."

Marianne turned her face away and stared out at the bustling throng of London traffic. When she eventually spoke her voice was thick with constraint. "You know, Helen, my father loved me very much and my Godfather, Sir William Kenneth, intended only kindness when he sponsored my admission to Miss Beale's academy. And yet, I have been forced to conclude that my father and Sir William between them managed to produce a monster."

"I cannot accept that, my dear Marianne. Pray recollect that you are talking of *my* best friend!"

Marianne touched her friend's arm gratefully. "I admit that your taste is usually perfect, but in this instance I'm afraid that friendship overclouds your judgment. I am a misfit, Helen, and I find my life often uncomfortable. My brother is a dear, good soul, but he does not understand more than half of what I say, and he approves of less than a quarter. Indeed, I suspect that my poor sister-in-law secretly believes me to be speaking Hindustani a fair proportion of the time! And yet *you* know that I shall never be acceptable to the aristocratic members of society. It is ludicrous to hope that the Earl will ever accept me for what I am . . . and without his wholehearted support, I shall be slighted by every member of the *haut ton*, and every lady in the countryside around his estates."

Miss Thatcher looked unhappy and did not attempt to deny the truth of Marianne's claims. "Would it not be better to explain your feelings to Mr. Perkins? He is an indulgent brother and would not force you into a marriage that you seriously disliked, I am sure."

"It is true that Thomas is kindness itself to me . . . on almost all occasions. On the subject of my marriage, however, he will not listen. He has been trying to find me an aristocratic husband ever since I returned from India, and now that he has actually discovered an *earl* who is willing to wed me, he can't understand that I do not particularly wish to become a countess." She shook her head impatiently.

"No, Helen. Reasoning with Thomas will do no good. I remember too clearly what happened on the occasion of my betrothal to Horace Johnson. My late husband was a good man but . . . but I could not bear to enter into another loveless marriage."

Miss Thatcher, who had watched the tribulations of her friend through two years of marriage in a foreign land, to a man thirty years her senior, could find nothing constructive to say. She finally attempted one last feeble remonstrance. "How can you be sure that the Earl will be sufficiently repelled to call off the match? If his financial straits are as desperate as you believe, presumably he will overlook all but the grossest impropriety."

Marianne spoke through tightly clenched lips. "We can at least make the attempt. If all else fails, I shall have to consider what I may do that is grossly improper."

"No, no!" Miss Thatcher raised her hands in mock despair. "Heaven forbid that I should encourage your mind to turn to even more unladylike scheming! I see that I have talked myself into the unhappy position of having to hope that your plot succeeds."

Marianne placed an affectionate arm around her friend's shoulders. "No wonder dear Thomas considers you of doubtful worth as a chaperone, Helen! Underneath that boringly righteous exterior developed after ten years with Miss Beale, I do believe there beats a heart which is scarcely less rebellious than my own!"

Miss Thatcher assumed an expression of spurious disapproval. "Let us not exaggerate, my dear Marianne. If you remember correctly, you will recall that it was you who invariably launched us all into trouble at Miss Beale's, and

I who was forced to risk my position as a teacher in order to rescue you."

"Ah, but now that I am a grim old widow of two-and-twenty, you may no longer hold such childish escapades against me. Confess that you would rather share a house with me in town, than find ourselves shut up in some stuffy mausoleum of a country mansion."

But Miss Thatcher was not to be drawn. She primmed her mouth, tried her best to look severe, and said chidingly, "Now Mrs. Johnson! We must both submit to Mr. Perkins' superior judgment. How many times had Miss Beale to tell us? The gentlemen *always* know best!"

"Miss Beale had wits enough to remove herself to an environment that totally excluded masculine wisdom. That is why she was able to persist in a belief about male intelligence that would have been dispelled after five minutes' exposure to a husband, a father or a brother."

Miss Thatcher was an optimist. "Perhaps you will find the Earl positively charming. You may even begin to regret that appalling purple satin."

Marianne descended from the carriage with a decidedly aggressive thump. "You are dreaming, Helen," she said. "I have already decided that the noble Earl and I will dislike one another excessively. It is not at all likely that I shall change my mind."

CHAPTER FOUR

Prothero opened the door of Mr. Perkins' townhouse with a dignity that would have sufficed for the entry of the Archbishop into Canterbury Cathedral. He bowed slightly to the two gentlemen waiting on the doorstep, noting the crested carriage that had brought them with an inner nod of satisfaction.

Despite the fact that he was now forced to perform his services in a regrettably inferior household, Prothero never failed to maintain the punctilious standards favoured by the noble families who had previously enjoyed his services. It had been with considerable reluctance that Prothero abandoned the household of Lord Roxdean some ten years previously, and the conclusion that regular wages were preferable to a noble name and ancient lineage had not been lightly reached. Employment with the improvident Lord Roxdean had been sadly exchanged for employment with Mr. Thomas Perkins who, though congenial and marvellously prompt with wages, would never manage to meet any of Prothero's exacting standards.

Mrs. Johnson, on the other hand, had been accorded the butler's full approval ever since her return from Miss Beale's Seminary. The rumour, currently sweeping the kitchen quarters, that Mrs. Johnson was about to marry no less a personage than the Earl of Tarrisbroke had caused a quiver of family pride to race through Prothero's ample frame.

He therefore inspected the Sunday afternoon visitors with minute attention, and was conscious of an unprecedented surge of exuberance when the elder visitor informed him that the Earl of Tarrisbroke and Mr. Cowper had come to keep their appointment with Mr. Perkins. Although no vestige of inner excitement was visible on Prothero's stolid countenance, in the few minutes that it took to summon the footman and divest the visitors of hats, gloves and canes, Prothero's nimble brain had catalogued every item of the gentlemen's appearance.

Mr. Cowper was swiftly dismissed as the lawyer and man of affairs that he evidently was, but Prothero swept an admiring eye over the commanding height of the Earl of Tarrisbroke, allowing his glance to linger approvingly on the starched frills of the Earl's evening shirt, the formal sobriety of knee breeches and silk stockings, the superbly fitting evening coat, and the single diamond fob that hung from his lordship's satin waistcoat. The Earl was evidently expected at a formal dinner on the other side of town, and Prothero's bosom swelled with pride. *These* were the sort of visitors to appreciate a properly run household.

Mr. Cowper and the Earl were ushered into the drawing room, where they discovered Mr. Perkins unhappily perched at the extreme edge of his chair. The truth of the matter was that Mr. Perkins had never before been introduced to an earl, and he had spent a miserable afternoon contemplating his approaching role as host and prospective brother-in-law to such an exalted member of the peerage. His instinctive kindness, which normally made every guest feel welcome, was paralysed under an oppressive sensation of nervousness.

Mr. Cowper summed up the situation at a glance, and since he was only too well aware that the Earl was even more embarrassed by the whole meeting than Mr. Perkins, he did his best to smooth over the introductions with harmless remarks about the weather and the general unhappy state of the government. These were two safe topics, he felt sure, since the entire population, regardless of social class, could be relied upon to unite in condemning each with an almost equal fervour.

The Earl finally relaxed sufficiently to apologise, in frigid tones, for the formality of his attire. "I am invited to dinner at Madame de Lieven's house, and I felt there would be insufficient time to change. I must beg your forgiveness for the inappropriate nature of my attire."

Thomas Perkins, who had until that moment not realized that there was anything at all strange about an earl who paid late afternoon calls in satin knee breeches, was so impressed by this casual reference to one of the august patronesses of the noted Almack's, that he was rendered entirely speechless. The vista of social joys opening up to his little Marianne seemed to be truly endless.

He finally recovered his voice sufficiently to offer his guests some refreshment, and to Mr. Cowper's relief, the excellent burgundy relaxed both of his charges—for so he had begun to consider them—to the point where they exchanged four or five harmless sentences without the need of his intervention.

After the second glass of burgundy, Mr. Perkins felt fortified enough to broach the topic that was uppermost in everybody's mind, and after clearing his throat several times, managed to enquire if his lordship wished to pursue the idea of a union between their two families.

The Earl winced slightly at the turn of phrase, but bowed with formal politeness and murmured that he had been honoured to learn that Mr. Perkins was prepared to consider his proposals. Since he was unable to bring himself to say anything further, it was left to Mr. Cowper to bridge the unfortunate gap in the conversation. This he did most efficiently by assuring Mr. Perkins that the general outline of the proposed marriage contracts had been entirely acceptable to his lordship.

Mr. Perkins, who found the Earl's icy formality of manner the personification of all that he had ever hoped for in a noble brother-in-law, was hard put to conceal his jubilation. His aplomb totally restored, he immediately launched into a description of his sister's manifold perfections. He simultaneously rang the bell for the butler, and sent Prothero, quivering with suppressed excitement, to request Marianne's presence in the drawing-room. With a clumsy attempt at tactfulness, he insisted upon removing Mr. Cowper to the library.

"I am sure, my lord, that you will prefer to meet my little sister alone," said Mr. Perkins with smiling bonhomie. "And I know you will not wish to bother your head poring over documents, my lord, for I'm sure all the figures would be right out of the line of your understanding."

His lordship was by now too sunk in gloom to pay the slightest heed to this unflattering estimate of his abilities, and merely nodded briefly as Cowper and Perkins retired to the comfort of the study. His thoughts concerning the proposed marriage had hovered between grim resignation and outright rebellion for the past three days, and Mr. Perkins' cheerfully plebian manners seemed to confirm his worst forebodings.

Nothing, however, had quite prepared him for the spectacle that Mrs. Johnson presented when she whirled into the drawing-room. The Earl found it almost impossible to form any accurate impression of her natural appearance, since her face was very obviously painted and her body was encased—there was no other word for it—in a gown of outrageous purple-striped satin. The stiff fabric, which had been out of fashion for at least a decade, stood out in formal pleats about her person. Black velvet bows deliberately scattered around the hem caught up the dress to reveal layers of lavender lace. The extraordinarily low cut of the bodice was mercifully veiled slightly by a foaming white lace fichu, and the whole disastrous *ensemble* was completed by an elaborate coiffure of wildly looped black curls, liberally interlaced with strings of amethysts.

In normal circumstances the Earl was a man of shrewd judgment, and the theatricality of the outfit would in itself have warned him of something seriously amiss. In this instance, however, Mrs. Johnson's appearance merely confirmed his darkest and most desolate fears, and he watched her approach in appalled silence, rooted to the ground by the strength of his misery.

Marianne had time to cast only one look at the haughty countenance, and immediately registered the Earl's disdainful expression while quite failing to notice the bleak misery reflected in his eyes. Perversely aware of a flash of anger—

her costume had, after all, been purchased with the intention of provoking precisely the reaction that now enraged her—she tripped into the room, hands drammatically outstretched, eyelashes fluttering in false modesty. She had even thought to provide herself with a fan.

"La, my lord, I'm sure I'm delighted to make your acquaintance." She peeped coquettishly out from behind the extended fan. "I've been on pins and needles to see your lordship ever since my brother first told me what a lucky girl I was going to be. 'What? Me a Countess?' I said. 'Well, Mr. Johnson would never have believed it, me and him never having moved very much in the best circles.' But our Thomas has arranged it all. He promised my Papa he'd look after me, and now you can see he's doing me right proud."

She faltered and fell silent as the Earl's absolute rigidity penetrated the screen of her assumed volubility. His face appeared a stone study in utter contempt. It required all her courage to approach him more closely, fluttering her fan and enveloping them both in waves of amber perfume. "La, but your lordship shouldn't let me prattle on, but then my dear sainted Mama was always used to say that when I'm excited there's no stopping my prattle, and I've been that excited this week that our Thomas has hardly been able to get a word in edgewise. It's not every day that you hear you're going to be a Countess, you know."

The Earl's vocal paralysis finally ended in an explosion of anger. "I was not aware, Madame, that I had as yet had the opportunity to lay any proposals for our marriage before you." With icy disdain he added, "In the circles I normally frequent, it is customary for the gentleman to suggest marriage to the lady—whatever the realities of the case—it is normally considered expedient to make no reference to the financial settlements which may accompany those proposals."

Marianne moved a little further away. Inwardly she seethed at the cold superiority of his words, and her heart contracted somewhat irrationally at the scorn he was no longer attempting to conceal. Innocently she stared at him from violet eyes. "Oh la, my lord, I'm sorry if I've offended you, I'm sure. I shall always be happy to adjust my behaviour to any standard your lordship wants. Mr. Johnson always told me that he'd never met such an obliging little girl as me. Was your lordship wishful of making me a declaration in form? I was just prattling on, thinking your lordship might have difficulty in finding the right words, not being overly acquainted with me. But then, we simple folks don't have a way with words like you—fancy, a proper peer of the realm!" she smiled with false joviality, and said confidingly, "I expect you've been taught to wrap your dirty linen up handsome right from the cradle." She fluttered the fan aimlessly about her folds of fichu, and then perched herself carelessly in a chair, making no particular effort to hide the expanse of shapely ankle that emerged from beneath the frills of lavender lace.

At any other time the Earl would have pursued his faint feelings of suspicion concerning the outrageous vulgarity of his destined bride. He knew that she had attended Miss Beale's Academy for more than a year, and she could not have survived a single week at that select establishment with a manner as grotesquely coarse as that she was now presenting for his delectation. But as it was, common sense had vanished completely under the stress of circumstance, and he literally closed his eyes against the purple-striped nightmare that lolled on the edge of his vision.

After years of exile in Europe, he had dreamed secretly of his return to England and his re-admission to the society of his birth. He had even hoped to find some woman with whom he could share his deeply-rooted love for the lands of Tarrisbroke and his wide understanding of the volatile politics of Europe. Now all such dreams lay in ruins at the feet of this over-painted, underbred woman.

Choked by feelings of repugnance at the price he was paying for his father's gross self-indulgence, he gritted his teeth and turned to face Mrs. Johnson. Unless he acted now, he knew his courage would fail him completely and—whatever the consequences to his mother and sister—no marriage would ever take place with this hideous widow. After ten years of neglecting his mother's interests, he could not allow his personal feelings to control his actions. The effort of speaking civilly forced the words out of his throat in a harsh parody of his normally concise tones.

"My friend Mr. Cowper has been good enough to inform me, Madam, that you would be prepared to entertain the idea of marriage with me. May I request the honour . . . Madam . . . of your hand in marriage?"

His words fell into a pool of appalled silence as Marianne realized the impasse to which she had brought herself. For the past three days she had fixed in her mind exclusively on the need to disgust the Earl from the moment of their first meeting. The possibility that the Earl would make her an unconditional offer of marriage at their first meeting had simply not occurred to her. She had assumed all along in making her plans that the Earl would want the financial settlements signed and fully agreed upon before committing himself to a formal declaration. How foolish she had been not to consider that his financial straits might be so desperate that he would ignore a degree of coarseness that ought to repel even the least sensitive of mortals.

But now—bitter irony!—she was trapped in the role she had herself created, for how could the gushing, vulgar and flirtatious Mrs. Johnson possibly refuse the proposal for which she appeared to have been angling? She stood up and walked across to the tall windows, turning her back upon the Earl. "Your lordship's proposals do me too much honour," she said sardonically, quite forgetting her new character in the stress of the moment.

The sudden change in voice and manner certainly escaped the Earl's notice. No doubt, thought Marianne with a fresh spurt of irrational anger, he considered a refusal so unlikely that his attention had already moved on to more important matters.

"Your acceptance makes me very . . . happy," said the Earl with extreme formality. His gaze seemed to be fixed on the wall-sconce to the left of Marianne's shoulders. "You will forgive me, I trust, if I beg leave to depart on a pressing engagement. I believe we may safely leave all further arrangements in the capable hands of Mr. Perkins and my lawyer."

"La, my lord, I see our meetings are to be short and sweet," she simpered. "But never fear, I'll be ready and waiting whenever you decide to tie the knot." Marianne shook out the rustling skirts of her gown taking a vicious pleasure in the look of bleak resignation that seemed permanently settled on to the Earl's face. "A wedding's always a good time for a bit of fun, and it'll be nice to have an excuse to buy a few new clothes. I'm powerful fond of purple."

A look of horror momentarily dissipated the stony rigidity of the Earl's expression. He inclined his head in a slight bow. "It has been a . . . pleasure . . . Madam, to make your acquaintance."

"Why likewise, my lord. Likewise, I'm sure."

CHAPTER FIVE

Neither the Earl nor Marianne was easily reconciled to the idea of their rapidly aproaching nuptials. The Earl insisted upon re-examining all the papers relating to his father's financial affairs, and only agreed with Mr. Cowper's gloomy prognostication of total ruin after an exhaustive exploration of all possible means of compounding interest, redeeming debts and extending mortgages. He closed the final, awesome ledger that showed the sum total of his father's debts with a look of defeat that touched the granite edges of Mr. Cowper's normally flinty heart.

"Come, your lordship," he said cheerfully. "The case is not altogether desperate. Mr. Perkins is an honest and engaging fellow, even if a little less . . . cultured . . . than we might wish. Mrs. Johnson is also young and charming. There must have been many a love-match that turned out less well than this marriage and that I'll warrant you."

The Earl looked at his lawyer warily. He had always considered Mr. Cowper a man of refined taste as well as a man of sound financial judgement. If, however, he could term the outrageous Mrs. Johnson "charming" then his taste—even his basic common sense—must surely be questionable. Feeling very much like a sane man let loose upon an island of bedlamites, the Earl inclined his head in polite acknowledgment of Mr. Cowper's remarks. His expression altered not one whit, however, as he said in constrained tones, "It is clearly hopeless to carry on expecting a miracle. I should be obliged if you would arrange the ceremony as soon as may be possible. I do not care for any of my family to be present, but I shall post down to Kent in order to alert them to the prospect of a bridal visit in the near future. I can no doubt be back in London within the week, if you can arrange a ceremony so soon."

"I am sure we shall find Mrs. Johnson very ready to accommodate your lordship in the matter of an early marriage. I know her brother is anxious to return to the supervision of his interests in Manchester, and Mrs. Johnson can only look forward to the moment when she becomes your bride." He beamed with comfortable sentimentality. Mrs. Johnson had seemed a nice enough little thing, quiet and unassuming. It was good to know that he had had a hand in working such a marvellous change in her circumstances.

The Earl could not prevent the sarcasm that coloured his voice. "We shall, I am sure, find Mrs. Johnson all eager compliance."

"Well, my lord, you may take off to visit the Dowager Countess and Lady Eleanor with an easy mind. I shall have all in train for a happy conclusion by the moment of your return."

The Earl, anxious to avoid contact with former friends, and equally anxious to renew his acquaintance with his mother and sister, posted down to his estates in Kent where he found everything in the worst possible state of disorder. Despite all Mr. Cowper's warnings, he had not previously realized the extent of his father's depredations, and he viewed the neglected lands with a rage that would have boded ill for the late earl had he been alive to observe it.

The Dowager Countess greeted him with copious tears and a depressing quantity of trailing black veils, and his sister Eleanor seemed determined to succumb to the vapours every time she thought about the forthcoming union of an Earl of Tarrisbroke with a woman whose family had been involved in Trade.

The Earl tried to sympathize with the noble refinement of his sister's feelings, but he found himself wishing with increasing frequency that Lady Eleanor's sensibilities could have been a little less nice, and his mother's demeanour a trifle less lachrymose. He could not quite suppress the conviction that rather more action over the past ten years, and rather less silent suffering, would have proven of immeasurable benefit to the Tarrisbroke Estates.

He returned to town at the end of the week almost as glad for an excuse to leave the noble refinements of Tarrisbroke Hall as he had been a week earlier to escape from the cheerful vulgarity of Mrs. Johnson. He took refuge in the lodgings of his friend Giles Packenham, and proceeded to make a concerted effort to drain that gentleman's cellar of brandy. He simultaneously mused aloud upon the impossibility of finding females who were not either mercenary leeches, intolerable vulgarians or unbearable masses of sensitivity.

Mr. Packenham kindly agreed with all these strictures upon the opposite sex, and proved himself the truest of friends by remaining sufficiently sober to deliver his charge, properly attired and rather pale, to St. George's, Hanover

Square in good time for the wedding.

Meanwhile, Marianne had not been idle, but her repeated protestations had fallen upon deaf ears. Mr. Perkins listened to his sister's arguments with no more than half his attention, his mind full of entrancing day dreams that saw him received in Tarrisbroke Castle (he felt quite sure his lordship would eventually have a castle) as an honoured guest of the delightfully haughty Earl. Nothing would convince him that Marianne's protests were anything more than the freakish whims of a typically disordered female mind.

The accumulated evidence of the past twenty-two years, which showed quite plainly that his sister's mind was neither freakish nor disordered, was not allowed to interfere with this highly satisfactory conclusion. Just as she had been on the occasion of her marriage to the late Mr. Johnson, Marianne found herself utterly defeated.

She eventually retired to her room and indulged in a storm of hysterical weeping that inspired Miss Thatcher with genuine fears for her health, and caused Mr. Perkins to remark triumphantly that he had said all along that Marianne was suffering from nothing more than a typically feminine attack of the vapours. All this, he said happily, would be quite cured once little Marianne found herself a countess.

The absolute uselessness of resistance finally brought Marianne to a grudging acceptance of her destiny. She ceased to complain to her brother Thomas, answered all his questions in tones of dutiful compliance, and tried to fill her days with brisk walks in the Park and frequent visits to Madame de Blanchard's salon. There she purchased an array of bridal clothes that gladdened the heart of the modiste, and restored Mrs. Johnson to the pinnacle of respect where she had formerly resided. The noble indifference with which Mrs. Johnson learned the outrageous prices of her chosen gowns almost served to restore Madame's faith in the basic goodness of human nature.

The delivery of endless boxes and packages did nothing to alleviate the misery Marianne felt when left alone each night in her bedchamber, but at least she could console herself with the thought that her sorrow would be cloaked in a dazzling variety of fashionable garments. She struggled to put away childish dreams of love and companionship, and concentrated her thoughts on the prospect of having children upon whom to lavish her great stores of affection and interest.

The arrival from Manchester of Mrs. Martha Perkins, a much loved and kindly sister-in-law, encouraged Marianne in her new and calmer acceptance of the future. It was hard to remain altogether unimpressed by the advantages of becoming a countess, when Martha spent all day every day complimenting her upon her good fortune with unceasing and entirely genuine goodwill.

Miss Thatcher did her best to bolster this happier view of the forthcoming marriage, and by dint of concentrating on the many months of each year when Marianne would probably be left to her own devices, and much glossing over the details of the life Marianne might be expected to lead when the Earl of Tarrisbroke was in residence, she managed to send Marianne to St. George's, Hanover Square, on the appointed day in a tolerably composed frame of mind.

The Earl, who was already waiting at the chancel steps

with Mr. Packenham and Mr. Cowper, greeted the unmistakable sounds of his bride's arrival with awful resignation. Mentally he steeled himself to support the spectacle of his bride tripping down the aisle of the church arrayed in satin, artificial flowers and copious layers of lace veiling. In the end, his courage failed him and unable to tolerate the sympathy he imagined to be lurking behind the Honourable Giles Packenham's solemn expression, he did not turn to observe the advance of the bridal party, staring instead with fixed concentration at the Bishop, a Tarrisbroke great-uncle, who was performing the ceremony.

As she proceeded down the aisle of the church on the arm of her beaming brother, Marianne had ample opportunity to observe the powerful shoulders of the Earl, neatly shrouded in a coat of blue superfine. Hard as she tried to maintain her feelings of dutiful resignation, she felt a spurt of fierce anger as she contemplated the obstinately averted gaze of her bridegroom. It would serve him right, she thought irately, if she had allowed her imagination full reign and had turned up in puce satin like her sister-in-law.

The service proceeded without any noticeable hitch, despite the unwillingness of the bride and groom to look at each other. And if Marianne's voice trembled a little that was considered only proper in a bride, although perhaps somewhat surprising in a lady who had already been married.

Martha Perkins wept tears of unashamed joy, looking with considerable longing at the subdued elegance of her sister-in-law's pale blue silk gown and matching bonnet. The rigidly haughty expression of the Earl—already described to her in awed tones by Mr. Perkins—fulfilled every wish in regard to the person of the bridegroom, and had she not been so very well content with her own lot, Martha decided that she would have been full of envy at the thought of dear Marianne's happy future.

Miss Thatcher, who was privileged to know Marianne rather better than the other members of the wedding party, recognized immediately that the tremor in the bride's responses sprang from inadequately suppressed anger rather than maidenly modesty, and looking at the groom's unapproachable hauteur of manner she could sympathize only too readily with her friend. Neither bride nor groom looked to be of a placid or yielding disposition, and she acknowledged a quiver of anxiety as she thought of their life together.

The brief service was soon completed. The Earl raised the hand of his new wife to his lips and just brushed the tip of her fingers in a chaste salute. Mrs. Perkins sighed sentimentally. Thomas Perkins looked pleased at such noble reticence, and Marianne scowled.

It was precisely at this moment that the Earl glanced up for the first time and observed the fierce dislike that filled Marianne's eyes. He was too astonished to reflect on the meaning of this, and concentrated his attention instead upon the remarkable improvement in her clothes. He made a mental resolution, not very clearly formulated because of the residual effects of too much brandy, that he would personally supervize his wife's entire wardrobe from now on. He must make sure that they started married life as he intended to carry on. His wife might be responsible for the money that kept Tarrisbroke functioning, but *his* would be the commands that set events in motion.

The bishop and his secretary were introduced to the assembled guests and then departed with a considerable degree of pomp, having refused all the offers of hospitality pressed upon them by an excited Thomas Perkins.

It had mightily offended this good man's notions of what was right and proper for his little sister that the wedding should be such a miserly affair. He well remembered the marvellous opulence that had marked her marriage to Horace Johnson, and he had hoped to outdo even that stellar performance on this accasion. But he had been forced to resign himself to what Mr. Cowper termed 'a private ceremony' on being reminded that his lordship was recently bereaved and thus not able to indulge in any but the most modest of celebrations.

Mr. and Mrs. Perkins had therefore reluctantly prepared as simple a wedding breakfast as their pride would allow, which meant that the dining room of the Perkins townhouse groaned under a supply of hearty food and expensive delicacies that would comfortably have provided sustenance for a wedding party of fifty hungry people. Neither the Earl nor the new Countess of Tarrisbroke availed themselves of very much of this food, but the Earl made up for his omission by consuming inordinate amounts of Mr. Perkins' best burgundy and an even larger quantity of Mr. Perkins' best champagne.

The Countess was not seen to sip anything more intoxicating than a glass of water, and she remained exceptionally silent. Thomas Perkins, who had lived in lively dread of what his sister might actually do on her wedding day, considered this bashful silence just as well, and with willing assistance from Miss Thatcher and Mr. Packenham they contrived to create the impression that both the newly-weds were behaving just as they ought.

Such a happy pretence could not be continued indefinitely, however. Mr. Cowper, whose training as a lawyer made it difficult for him to ignore evidence that was plainly before his eyes, eventually deemed it advisable to get the couple started on their travels while his lordship was still moderately in command of his senses. He enquired innocently where the Earl planned to take his countess for their bridal journey, and an awful silence immediately descended upon the guests, as it became apparent to them all that the Earl had neglected to make any arrangements whatsoever for the start of his married life.

Mr. Packenham, once again proving himself a true friend in an hour of need, sprang into the breach. "Rodbourne House!" he exclaimed. "That is to say, I expect you are planning to stay in town this evening, Quentin? You would not like to arrive in Kent when you are exhausted, and the Dowager Countess will no doubt be expecting you tomorrow evening."

The Earl flashed his friend a look of profound thankfulness, and made valiant efforts to drag his addled brain back into action. "Yes ... no ... of course not. You are quite right, Giles. Lady Tarrisbroke and I will spend tonight in town."

The party heaved a small sigh of relief that this small episode had been brushed through without social disaster, but the Earl's alcohol-clouded senses did not realize that it was best to leave well enough alone. "Now what the devil are we going to do all evening?" He beamed happily, struck by a sudden thought. "Yes," he said. "We shall go to the theatre tonight. There's a new play at Covent Garden." He fixed somewhat blurred eyes upon Giles Packenham. "Come with us. Tarrisbroke box. All of you invited."

Mr. Packenham was appalled by this dreadful revelation of indifference to convention and made haste to protest the arrangements. His hesitant remarks were not at first heeded save by Mr. Cowper, since Mr. and Mrs. Perkins, whose ideas of aristocratic life encompassed vivid pictures of constant entertainment and very little down-to-earth daily living, found nothing strange in the suggestion that the Earl and his bride would wish to spend the first evening of their marriage in the company of a large party at a public play. After repeated protestations from Mr. Packenham, however, wiser counsels finally prevailed, and the party broke up with most of the participants feeling that all had proceeded better than might have been expected.

Only the two principals entered the barouche that was to carry them across the town in moods of deepest depression. The Earl was uncomfortably aware that he had consumed far too much wine and—far from lightening his mood—the alcohol was in danger of sinking him into black despair.

Marianne was fighting a losing battle with her temper and trying hard not to dwell upon the fact that her noble husband was evidently not only a wastrel and a libertine but a drunkard as well. She was trying even harder, and without marked success, not to dwell upon the fact that drunk or sober, the Earl's hard eyes and satirical expression exerted a fascination that poor Mr. Johnson—for all his manifold virtues—had never hoped to achieve.

CHAPTER SIX

The Earl and Countess of Tarrisbroke were relieved to learn that the staff of Rodbourne House felt more than capable of providing a dinner for the new Countess, despite the fact that no warning had been given of her impending arrival. The Earl, having delivered his instructions concerning dinner with a supreme disregard for the difficulties attendant upon procuring quail and fresh lobster in the centre of town an hour before the meal, bowed with exaggerated courtesy over his wife's hand and retreated to his rooms in order to nurse a headache of increasingly monumental proportions.

Left standing alone in the great hallway, Marianne was forced to conclude that her husband considered his duties towards her fully discharged, and she was grateful to retire to a suite of rooms tactfully recommended by the housekeeper. Having paced several times up and down the faded Persian carpet and thrown her bonnet at the fly-blown looking-glass, she tried to decide whether to develop a case of strong hysterics or to collapse on her bed, never again to get up.

In the end, she resisted temptation and followed neither course, simply sending for her maid and requesting with her usual pleasant manner some assistance in dressing for dinner. Unfortunately, Becky was overwhelmed by the faded glories of her new surroundings and instead of carrying on her usual aimless but gossipy monologue, she helped her mistress dress in a repressed and respectful silence.

Thus deprived of any distractions, Marianne was at liberty to examine her own feelings and quickly discovered herself to be in a state of total, helpless fury. Normally sensitive to the problems of those around her, Marianne tonight did not want to burden her mind with questions about the state of her husand's emotions. It would have been difficult even for a dispassionate observer to recognize that the Earl was himself a hostage to destiny, and Marianne was neither dispassionate nor anxious to be charitable. Consequently, she arrived punctually at the dining table, exquisitely coiffed and gowned, outwardly calm, but inwardly a seething mass of unresolved hostilities.

The first course had been fully served before the Earl emerged from behind the misery of his aching head long enough to take accurate note of his surroundings. His glance flickered briefly over the familiar furnishings of a room he had known since childhood, before coming to rest apprehensively upon the face of his new wife.

The Earl shook his head silently once or twice, as if to make sure that clouds of champagne were no longer affecting his powers of observation, but the same profile of classic perfection greeted his startled gaze. He craned his neck in order to remove a large and singularly unattractive epergne from his line of sight, and stared again at the perfectly symmetrical nose, the high white forehead and the long slender neck of his countess.

"Do you wish for some particular dish, my lord?" His

wife's voice, cool and quietly amused, floated down the absurd length of the table.

"Dish? Er . . . no. No thank you. He lapsed into an unhappy silence and abandoned his efforts to reconcile this vision of loveliness with the mincing Mrs. Johnson whom he had met not ten days previously. While his wife calmly helped herself to a dish of scallops, he ran a connoisseur's eye over her outfit. She was wearing a pale yellow gauze overdress with a silk slip dyed in a deeper shade of the same colour. She seemed to be entirely without paint on her face, although the creamy pallor of her complexion seemed so perfect that he wondered if the candlelight was deceiving him. She was certainly not wearing any jewellery, however, other than a small diamond tiara that held back the severe coils of her hair, piled in dramatic curls of dark brown high on her head.

Her outfit, the Earl decided, compared very favourably with Maria Gabriella at her best, and his wife had even avoided the temptation of gilding the lily by adding quantities of shimmering jewels.

The Earl of Tarrisbroke blinked hard and tried to think of something to say. His wife forestalled him, however.

"This is excellent chicken, is it not? We must remember to express our thanks to your cook for his efforts."

"Yes." For the life of him, the Earl could not think of anything else he could suitably say.

The Countess smiled kindly. "It is now your turn to introduce a topic of conversation, my lord. That is the way it is done with married couples, you know."

"I bow to your superior experience, Madam."

"Well, yes. That is probably a very sound notion. You

see, I have already had two years of training."

"I hardly think, Madam, that your years with Mr. Johnson will have equipped you with conversation suited to your new station in life."

"No," said Marianne, with seeming equanimity. "You are probably right. Mr. Johnson was a particularly kind person and therefore instinctively courteous. I can quite see that he lacked all the natural advantages of . . . noble . . . manners. No doubt indifference to the feelings of those around you has to be taught from birth?" Her sweet smile failed to reach the brilliant glitter of her eyes. "Would you agree with me, my lord?"

The Earl spoke curtly to the butler. "Lady Tarrisbroke and I wish to be alone. You may leave the dish of comfits and remove the other platters."

"Very good, my lord." The butler bowed with an impassive dignity. If he understood the import of the exchange that had just occurred, his face gave no indication of it. With a signal to the footmen, the remaining covers were lifted from the table, and the Earl and Countess of Tarrisbroke were left alone.

The Earl just managed to control his accumulated sense of grievance until the door closed behind the butler, then he turned to face his wife.

"Perhaps you would be good enough to explain the meaning of that silly masquerade you performed at the occasion of our first meeting?" Without waiting for a reply he ground out, "I shall not attempt to express my displeasure at your conduct in front of servants who have served this family for generations. I should be obliged, however, if you would inform me why you found it necessary to behave with such appalling vulgarity on the day that we met?"

Marianne responded with false lightness. "Why that is quite simply explained, my lord. I did not wish to marry you, and therefore hoped to dissuade you from pursuing a union that promised to prove distasteful to both parties."

The Earl was conscious of severely ruffled feelings, the more so because he found this new Marianne bewilderingly desirable. Although his affaires in Europe had all been conducted with experienced and willing married women, he had caused many a broken heart among the Italian and German debutantes, and had grown used to thinking his suit well-nigh irresistible. "I was not aware, Madam, that my proposals were obnoxious to you," he said stiffly. "I had been reliably informed—as I thought—that you looked with favour upon the match."

Marianne's voice was without inflexion. "I can well believe that you were misinformed concerning my wishes, my lord. On the subject of matrimony, I'm afraid that my brother finds it difficult—in fact, impossible—to distinguish between *his* wishes and *my* feelings."

"In your situation," said the Earl haughtily, "I should have thought marriage represented a change for the better."

"In my situation?" Marianne's voice was deceptively mild. "What was there especially in *my* situation that rendered marriage so desirable? For the past year I have enjoyed a considerable degree of independence and the company of an intelligent and kind-hearted friend. I had no inclination for changing my lot, and no thought at all that my life would be improved by marrying an earl whose reputation was already ... notorious."

The Earl rose to his feet and walked over to the great hearth, stirring the logs with the toe of his boot. He watched the shower of sparks falling to the ground and struggled unsuccessfully to retain control of his temper.

There was some excuse for the ragged state of his nerves. Within the space of five weeks he had been informed of his father's death and had travelled halfway across Europe on horseback. He had also faced up to the prospect of financial ruin and been forced to marry an unknown and unwanted woman.

He recognized, in a small rational corner of his brain, that he was in no fit state to make decisions that would affect the whole course of his married life but, as he stared into the embers of the fire he felt the frustrations of the past weeks coalesce into a burning resentment of the woman who was now his bride. Only one clear sensation surfaced from the muddled pool of his emotions—an unworthy but powerful desire to disturb the apparent calm of this adversary, to subdue her physically if he could not conquer her mentally.

At last he turned away from the fire and said brusquely, "We are married now, and the reasons why this happened need no longer trouble us. God knows, there is nothing that we can do to repair the damage." He walked over to Marianne's side and pulled her to her feet. He placed his hand firmly beneath her chin and forced her to turn up her face for his inspection. Marianne's long lashes fell immediately over the dark violet of her eyes, veiling her expression, and the Earl drew in a sudden sharp breath.

His grip on her arms tightened cruelly and he gave a

short laugh. "I suppose I should be grateful that you look as you do, and not as I once feared. At least it will make the provision of an heir for Tarrisbroke a more interesting task." He forced himself to ignore the tremors that ran through her body, and bent his head to kiss her mouth, his eyes burning with a potent mixture of anger and desire. His lips hardly touched her cheek, however, before he felt the stinging impact of her hand striking his face.

"You should strive to remember my bourgeois background, my lord," she said in a shaking voice. "The daughters of tradesmen are not accustomed to being treated as ... as ... women of easy virtue. Our chastity is too valuable a commodity to be lightly given away."

The Earl looked at her with contempt, touching the livid welts left by her fingers on the pallor of his face. "I am not likely to forget the details of your background," he said bitingly. "But at some stage you must learn to behave as if you were born a lady, so it may as well be now. Permit me to remind you that we *are* married, and your moral scruples thus seem singularly out of place."

"But we do not know one another," protested Marianne, pulling herself away from his side.

The Earl smiled sarcastically. "I have just suggested the ideal solution to that problem, my dear. Pray do not subject me to any more examples of the methods you have previously employed to protect your virtue." Before she could offer any further protest, she found herself locked in his arms, her head crushed against the starched muslin frills of his shirt. Then, just as suddenly, she was pushed gently away as the sounds of a booming voice penetrated the thick oaken doors of the dining salon.

"It seems that you have a respite before we—er—further our acquaintance," said the Earl. "I believe we have just heard my uncle's voice, although I cannot understand what he is doing here."

The doors opened even as he spoke, and Marianne was able to observe her husband clutched in the enthusiastic grasp of a tall, thin man, whose lugubrious expression was belied by the hearty joviality of his voice.

"Quentin, you young rascal, it's good to see you! Forgive the call at this hour, but I had not time to stand on ceremony. I have to be off again to Brussels on Friday. Thank God you hadn't sloped off to Tarrisbroke!"

He stepped back and gave the Earl's arm a second enthusiastic pumping. "And what's all this tarradiddle Trimble was telling me about the Countess? Knew your mother couldn't be in town . . . stands to reason with the sad state of affairs. . . . Yes, Well. Least said about your father, the better. Just want you to know, m'boy, that if you need assistance, you've only to tell me."

He looked at the Earl's tense expression, and chuckled good-humouredly. "You may as well remove that haughty look from your face, my dear nephew, and tell me how your father's affairs *really* stand. Couldn't get a word out of that miserable stick of a lawyer the last time I tried to talk to him." Sir Henry paused finally for breath, and the Earl drew him firmly away from the firelight and towards the shadowy length of the dining table.

"It is good to see you, sir, whatever the reason for your call. And despite the generosity of your offer, I am happy to say that my father's affairs stand in tolerable order." He smiled affectionately at his uncle, and warmth flooded his features. "No doubt Trimble mentioned the Countess because, knowing how you rattle on, he wished to alert you to the fact that I am not dining alone. The fact is, sir, that I was married this morning, and I now beg leave to present the new Countess of Tarrisbroke." He turned to Marianne and said briefly, "I should like to present to you my mother's brother, Sir Henry Lane."

Marianne rose from the table and dropped a graceful curtsy, but she was not allowed to complete the formal phrases of welcome. "What's this?" cried Sir Henry, sweeping her towards the brighter lights at the side of the room. "Married! And how come you to wed such a Beauty, Quentin, when you would have us all believe that you have not set foot in England these three years past?"

The Earl replied without inflexion. "My . . . wife . . . spent several years overseas, sir. We did not meet at one of London's fashionable parties as you might have supposed."

Sir Henry had not represented his Government's interests at the Court of Louis XVIII for nothing, and was perfectly capable of detecting an unspoken story behind his nephew's curt sentences. He smiled charmingly at the Countess, however, murmuring that London's loss had undoubtedly been the Continent's gain. He added cheerfully, "You are obviously a woman of high courage as well as superlative beauty, ma'am, if you are prepared to take on the arduous role of wife to my rapscallion of a nephew."

Marianne was grateful to him for his polished flow of compliments, and smiled at him warmly. "I am not sure that my courage rates so great a measure of praise! I have not yet spent one full evening in the Earl's company, and already I am wondering if I really knew the man I agreed to marry."

She saw that the Earl was listening to her words with an intentness that surprised her, and was annoyed to feel a delicate flush of colour creeping up to stain her cheeks. She looked at Sir Henry with eyes full of wry laughter. "I have, however, already learned one wifely lesson very well. I know when I must leave the gentlemen alone! You called upon my husband this evening because you have something of an urgent nature to disclose to him, so I shall leave you, Sir Henry, with my best wishes for a safe and comfortable journey to Brussels."

"I look forward to furthering our acquaintance, Lady Tarrisbroke." Sir Henry bowed once more over her outstretched hand. "I cannot deny that I require a few moments of my nephew's time, but I hope that your bridal journey may bring you into Belgium and that we may have the pleasure of entertaining you. It will be some weeks before I move on to St. Petersburg."

The Earl walked over to his wife's side, and spoke curtly as he escorted her to the door. "We leave early for Kent tomorrow, Madam. The journey is tiresome and some of the roads not very good, so I trust you will be able to rest well."

She raised dark violet eyes to meet his own. "Why thank you, my lord. I am looking forward to a night of *undisturbed* repose." He raised both her hands to his lips and allowed a slightly quizzical smile to flicker across his mouth. Hastily Marianne withdrew her fingers from his touch and said primly. "There is no need to offer your escort, my lord, for I see one of the footmen waiting to light me to my chamber. Do not worry that I shall oversleep. My own maid is with me and is accustomed to preparing me for an early start to the day."

She was conscious of a most unseemly desire to linger, and hastily, to cover her confusion said, "Your uncle, sir, is waiting for your presence."

"Alas, you are too right. Sleep well." He bowed with exquisite formality and turned back to face his uncle. "Now, sir, you see me ready to attend to you."

CHAPTER SEVEN

The door shut softly behind Marianne, and Sir Henry expelled his breath in a long sigh. "Well, Quentin, I'm not denying that I'm pressed for time—something devilish important to ask of you—but first of all, m'boy, you're going to tell me what all this is about. Married! And to somebody you never mentioned to me when I saw you last month!"

"Our marriage was only recently agreed upon sir, and will be announced in the *Post* tomorrow. I could not inform you of our intentions last month because I had no plans for matrimony at that time."

Sir Henry relaxed more comfortably in his chair and said imperturbably, "You may come down off your high ropes and remove that pokered-up expression from your face. If you don't wish to tell me why you married without a word of warning to your family, Quentin, then I'm not going to press you. But don't try and pretend to me that your father's financial foolishness had nothing to do with this, because I won't believe it. No! Don't bother to act the haughty Earl with me. Just pour me some of the port that I see sitting on the table over there, and let me tell you why I've come. I had better speak quickly, before you throw me out of the house."

The Earl laughed. "You must know there is very little likelihood that I shall attempt anything so undiplomatic as to throw you out. No matter how much I may wish you and your questions at the devil, I cannot afford to alienate the affections of so prominent a member of our government!"

Sir Henry shifted in his chair, sipping the mellow port with a sigh of contentment. "Ah, Quentin! There are times when I wish *myself* at the devil. . . . I'm getting too old for this constant racketing about the Continent. It is bad enough that I must set out to captivate the attention of the Russian Emperor and place one of Prinny's wilder schemes before him, but I had no sooner reached Brussels, en route for the Russias, you know, when word came that I was needed back here in London."

"If the purpose of your visit to me is to explain how you feel yourself out-of-place at the centre of political intrigue and government planning, then I regret to inform you that you have already failed in your mission. I have no doubt that your rackety old bones rejoiced in every jolt of the carriage and every heave of the boat. There can be few men in England whose advice is so much sought after and even—on rare occasions—acted upon. There are not many people, my dear uncle, who enjoy the confidence of the Prince *and* Wellington!"

"Well, well. I do my best to bring an element of common-sense into their schemes, you know." Sir Henry tried to look modest and failed lamentably. "But I have a job of work for you to undertake, Quentin, and the deuce of it is that I can't ask anybody else. It's not a request that I ought to make of somebody who hasn't yet managed to spend an evening alone with his new wife!"

"Since I perceive that you have every intention of asking me anyway, I suggest sir, that you unburden yourself of the whole."

Sir Henry poured himself a further helping of port and leaned forward in his chair. "I know that it's no news to you to hear that details of Government plans are forever being leaked to the French government—and to all the little European princelings who can be counted upon to make trouble. Ever since the war with America, Europe's been riddled with government agents, all looking to make a few golden guineas by peddling supposed government secrets." Sir Henry gave a sharp bark of laughter. "Most of the time, the information they sell isn't worth the scrap of paper it's written on, but every so often some damn fool who should know better will talk in front of his servants. And then if the servant needs money it's only a matter of time before the supposedly secret plans or information turn up in all the European capitals."

The Earl's attention was caught. "I had not realized that the safety of our military plans was still a cause for concern. I knew that some French emigrés created problems twenty years ago. And of course, those French aristocrats who chose to accept Napoleon's offer of safety and returned to France must have taken with them a great deal of information. But it is hard to believe, sir, that much important information is now crossing the Channel. Besides, we are at peace."

Sir Henry snorted contemptuously. "Officially we are at peace." Impatiently he snapped his fingers. "I would not care to wager a single bottle of good French brandy on the chances of our continuing that way for more than a couple of years. Europe—as you should know—is a pot ripe for boiling over."

The Earl inclined his head. "I cannot take your wager since I agree with you that the present peaceful state of Europe will not endure for long. But tell me, sir, why you are brought scrambling back to London because of security failures that have, I am sure, occurred regularly for the last thirty years?"

Sir Henry twisted uncomfortably. "There is every reason to suppose, from the nature of the documents that are now surfacing in Paris and some other cities, that the most important leaks of information are coming from my office. My personal staff includes several foreigners, young sprigs most of 'em, sent to learn the business of diplomacy by acting as aides or liaison officers between my office and their own governments. Unfortunately, the leakage of information seems to have been so wide-ranging that it is not even possible to say with certainty whether the informant is French, or German, or even some other nationality entirely. It is only certain that the spy, if he exists, is violently opposed to the rule of Louis XVIII." Sir Henry permitted himself a wry laugh. "As you can imagine, that does not precisely narrow my field of suspects."

He thought quietly for a while, before adding, "Of course, Louis XVIII has such an extraordinary capacity for allowing his supporters to make him look foolish, that it is not always possible to be quite sure that his diplomatic blunders are the result of deliberate manipulation rather than simple misjudgment. However, the conversations I have had since my return to London convince *me* absolutely that somebody who can gain access to my confidential papers is in the service of a hostile foreign government."

"I perceive the makings of a government scandal, perhaps even a political crisis, and I have no doubt that your counsel was urgently needed. I cannot think, however, that my very circumscribed understanding of the problems would aid anybody in any way."

Sir Henry gave a crack of laughter. "Lord, nobody wants your advice, Quentin. London's got more people standing around waiting to give their opinion on any and every subject than a meadow has blades of grass. I need you for a very practical purpose . . . I need you as a messenger."

"I am flattered." The Earl looked at his uncle with a touch of irony. "You do not care to tax me with too arduous a mental task?"

"I have never doubted your supply of brains, Quentin, merely your willingness to use them. However, you have not yet heard why I need your help. There is more to my story."

"I hardly dare ask to whom I am supposed to deliver this message? It must be to one of my European acquaintances?"

"Yes," said Sir Henry bluntly. "I am asking you to help me for two reasons. Firstly because I am sure that I can trust you completely, and secondly because it is well known in Europe that you are . . . intimately . . . acquainted with the Mazaretto family."

The Earl expelled his breath on a long sigh. "Now we reach the nub of the matter. Today I was married, but tomorrow you wish me to take a message to my former mistress! Have I guessed it? Indeed, what could be more charming!"

Sir Henry looked as close to total discomposure as was possible for a man of his nature and training, but he rallied immediately. "Naturally I had no notion that you were married when I came here this evening. But in fact it makes no odds. Of course I do not wish you to take anything to the *Principessa*."

"You relieve my mind. Do pray continue."

"Maria Gabriella's cousin, Prince Alberto, is complaining that he is receiving no support from our ministers or from the officers Wellington sent to help him get his army back on its feet. He's probably right at that. Old Stewart is too busy worrying about what Castlereagh is saying at Court to care how the army is faring in a remote part of the Adriatic." Sir Henry glared moodily at a falling log. "But the fact is, Quentin, we cannot afford to let King Louis' opponents gather strength. Boney may be imprisoned on Elba for the time being, but that doesn't mean we can afford to have all the minor princelings who are annoyed with the British Government turning over their half-baked armies to his supporters. In short, Quentin, we cannot afford to let Prince Alberto commit his soldiers to the French revolutionaries, and that is what he has been threatening to do. He is beginning to believe that such a move would offer him more protection against Metternich's Austrian armies than remaining loyal to us."

The Earl walked across the darkened room and stared out of the window on to the small London garden that glimmered in the ethereal light of a full moon. "I cannot pretend that the Prince's wavering loyalties come as a shock to me. I had suspected as much when Maria Gabriella was first ordered home from Paris, and the Prince's manner towards me once we were in Ancona confirmed my suspicions that the British were about to pass out of favour in his province. And so, my dear uncle, if I am supposed to persuade Prince Alberto that his future welfare depends on maintaining his alliance with England, I fear you have most certainly overrated my powers of persuasion. Not to mention the fact that I cannot feel my choice as an emissary of the Government would be altogether in the very best of taste."

"Quentin, marriage seems to have addled your wits. I do not expect you to carry political messages of a highly sensitive nature to the family of your ex-mistress! But I need you—and your notorious connection to the Mazaretto family—as a decoy in setting up my investigation. Refrain from interrupting me for a few moments, so that I may explain what I am trying to do which is, in effect, to bring down two birds with one stone."

"I am all silent attention," the Earl said dryly.

"A couple of years ago when our armies were pushing Boney back inland from the southern coast of France, Colonel Hendon's troops were involved in a skirmish with some renegade soldiers of Bonaparte. The Colonel captured a fair bit of treasure from the French soldiers, including the Crown of Saint Helen-Theodora which had been stolen from the Cathedral at Ancona. Perhaps you know that the peasants along the Adriatic coast regard her Crown as a holy relic?"

The Earl nodded briefly and remarked, "I'm sure that Prince Alberto's attitude is more practical."

Sir Henry shrugged. "Of course. The Prince regards it

merely as an excellent source of ready cash, and has asked the British Government to return it to him as a token of good faith. The sale of the rubies and diamonds in the Crown would probably raise sufficient funds for Prince Alberto to re-equip half his army. On the other hand, if the Crown falls into the possession of the revolutionaries, it could easily be used as a holy talisman to rally the peasants to their side. You will see how important it is for the British Government to ensure that the Crown is returned safely to Prince Alberto."

"I am, of course, flattered if you are suggesting that I should ride *ventre-à-terre* across Europe, clutching this Crown in my saddle-bags." The Earl's voice was apologetic. "It's not that I wish to downplay my prowess on horseback, nor even my love of the absurd, but I should have thought a couple of trustworthy officers and a troop of well-trained soldiers would have been the most logical method of getting such a treasure safely to Italy."

Sir Henry sighed. "You are correct, and the Crown was despatched in just the way you suggest earlier this evening. Nobody knows that this is the case, however, save I myself and now you, of course. Not even the officers know what they are carrying to Prince Alberto."

The Earl looked at his uncle in evident bewilderment. "Sir, I have spent the last five weeks since I heard of my father's death in a state of turmoil. I was married only this morning—not exactly a step to be undertaken lightly, I have discovered. It seems that I must confess that my mental powers are sadly depleted. If I am not to carry political messages, if my advice is not sought, if I am not needed as a porter for the Martyr's Crown what, in Heaven's name, do you wish me to do?"

Sir Henry rose to his feet and looked at his nephew with a touch of humour lurking behind his eyes. "I want you to accept a leather case from one of my secretaries tomorrow morning, and carry it with a great deal of pomp and circumstance to our Embassy in Brussels. I am intending to be exceptionally careless—in a most discreet way, of course—about where you are going and what is inside the leather case you are carrying." His voice acquired an uncharacteristically wistful note. "It is probably too much to hope that one of my aides will personally try to remove what he believes to be Saint Helen-Theodora's Crown. But at the very least, even if we do not discover the source of the leaks in my office, attention will be focused upon you and my troop of soldiers will have a greatly increased chance of arriving successfully in Ancona. Then, too, I am now on my guard, and I shall be able to watch the members of my staff with a fresh awareness. I do not altogether despair of somebody betraying undue interest in your movements."

The Earl paced the room for some minutes before he spoke. At last he turned to face his uncle. "Sir, leaving aside the question of whether I really wish to help Prince Alberto sell the jewels contained in a priceless religious relic, what you ask is impossible. I admit that a few months ago—even a few weeks ago—I might have welcomed the opportunity to sink my problems beneath the greater weight of a political emergency. But you must see, I am sure you will understand, that it is not possible to marry on one day and go chasing off to Brussels on the next!"

Sir Henry shot a surreptitious glance at his nephew from beneath discreetly lowered lids. "Well, I'm not saying that

I wasn't almost bowled over when I came in and discovered that my nephew—whom I had last seen in circumstances it is probably wiser not to recall—was now a sober married man. But as soon as you told me that Lady Tarrisbroke had travelled extensively abroad, it came to me in a flash that the case was not desperate."

The Earl eyed his uncle warily. "I am almost afraid to ask the meaning of your remarks."

"No, no! Nothing alarming, I assure you. Merely that it seems to me that your marriage need have little impact upon my plan. You and Lady Tarrisbroke met abroad, what could seem more natural than that you should travel back to the Continent for your nuptial voyage?"

The Earl laughed in disbelief. "You cannot expect your suspected revolutionaries to believe that I am carrying a priceless State treasure on my honeymoon! Sir, have you given any thought to the possible dangers of this task you wish me to undertake? Surely even the most credulous of foreign agents would find it hard to believe that I would expose my wife to the chance of such danger?"

Sir Henry looked embarrassed once more. "The thing is, Quentin, your dealings with women in the past have not led people to believe that your attitudes are basically *protective*."

The Earl interrupted coldly. "You speak of women whom I have known in the past. We are now discussing the Countess of Tarrisbroke—my wife."

Sir Henry cleared his throat. "Yes, well, I am aware that you make a distinction. I was merely answering your question as to how it might appear to other people. In fact, I cannot believe there is any danger either to you or to Lady Tarrisbroke, or I should not suggest the scheme to you. After all, we are dealing with sophisticated political manipulators, not revolutionary desperadoes. None of my aides is very likely to burst into Tarrisbroke Hall and demand the Crown at pistol-point."

"My dear uncle, you sound almost disappointed!"

"Well, you cannot deny that such an action would present me with irrefutable proof, and I am confident your servants would disarm the man before any damage could be done!"

"Next you will be telling me that Lady Tarrisbroke is to be congratulated at the delightful wedding journey we are planning for her. Come, sir! You are a married man and you must realize that one does not suggest a leisurely sojourn in Kent and suddenly alter this to a breakneck ride across the Continent of Europe without awakening some resentments in the bosom of one's bride."

Sir Henry regarded his nephew shrewdly. "I've had the pleasure of your acquaintance for over thirty years, Quentin, and I know it is useless to expect you to tell me the true facts behind this marriage of yours. I also took a good look at the determined thrust of your wife's chin, and I am prepared to guarantee that the next weeks will not be placid whether you spend them at Tarrisbroke or chasing across the Continent. Of course," he added hastily, "there is no need to tell Lady Tarrisbroke *why* you are going to Brussels. That might alarm her unnecessarily. Ladies' nerves are easily shattered, as you probably know better than I do, my boy. I have often wondered how you could stomach all that foreign emotion . . . too much for me, Quentin, and I have to admit it."

"I had better agree to your proposition, sir, before you threaten to throw the details of my unsavoury past before me." The Earl could not quite conceal the small thread of laughter that ran through his voice. "I suppose I have to say that the chance to make some small contribution towards maintaining the peace of Europe is not to be lightly thrown away."

Sir Henry sprang to his feet, the jovial words of enthusiasm in conflict with the expression of immeasurable relief that spread over his face. "Always knew I could count on you, Quentin. I shall send my secretary round to you tomorrow with the jewel case. Now I must give you all the instructions for meeting with me at the Ambassador's residence in Brussels, for we shan't be seeing one another before I leave."

"That is probably just as well," said the Earl. "I feel that more than *one* of your urgent missions would be quite beyond my powers to accomplish. Now that I am a married man, you must know that it is my expressed intention to retire to Tarrisbroke and grow turnips."

Sir Henry allowed his quizzing glass to travel the length of his nephew's immaculate evening clothes. "Hmmm. . . ." he murmured. "I can see that you have selected a future which is ideally suited to your natural tastes and talents. Not to mention how perfectly I imagine Lady Tarrisbroke would adapt to the life."

The Earl laughed. "I refuse to be provoked. *First* I shall pretend to deliver your Crown and *then* I shall retire to grow my turnips."

Sir Henry was at his most dignified. "You had better ring for Trimble," he said austerely. "If I am to write you a letter of introduction to our Ambassador we shall need pens and paper not to mention a few more lights. Don't worry, I shall not hold you much longer from your bed."

The Earl tugged at the bell-rope and turned a bland face towards his uncle. "Do not hurry yourself, my dear uncle. The night is still relatively young, and my time is *entirely* at your disposal."

"Then you are more of a fool than I thought you to be," said Sir Henry gruffly. "And don't bother to look daggers at me because I'm too old and too important to be knocked down, and even you wouldn't be crass enough to challenge me to a duel. There are some compensations in encroaching old age, after all."

The Earl fought down several angry and largely irrational retorts that might have been made to his uncle. It was not, perhaps, that gentleman's fault that the Earl had been politely but firmly told to stay out of his wife's bedroom. So far, the Earl had not even fully admitted to himself that he wished to let himself in. He walked across the room and tugged savagely at the bell-rope once again. "Trimble will be with us in a moment, uncle. Now tell me what route you suggest I should take in order to deliver this heirloom?"

CHAPTER EIGHT

The Earl rode beside his wife's travelling carriage in a mood of totally irrational irritation. Marianne, informed of the change in plans over the breakfast table, had accepted the news with the utmost placidity. She agreed to the Earl's suggestion that they might find Kent damp and depressing at this time of year with a polite inclination of the head, and he had been left nourishing the unflattering conviction that his wife had not believed a single word of his rambling explanations.

In the end he had been unable to tolerate Marianne's calm perusal of the *Morning Post* any longer, and he had flung his chair back from the table with considerable venom. "Indeed, ma'am, I had anticipated arousing slightly more curiosity with this sudden change of plans. I am happy to see that you are already resigned to such dutiful domestic submission."

Marianne looked up at him and allowed her eyes to become round with surprise. "You *wished* me to plague you with questions? Indeed, sir, since I am not altogether without wits, it was perfectly clear to me that our plans had been changed because of some request made to you by your uncle last evening. Should I tease you until you reveal his news to me?"

The Earl found himself uncomfortably trapped in a device of his own fashioning, for he could think of nothing to do in the face of this frontal attack other than mutter "My uncle?" in bewildered accents that deceived neither himself nor his wife.

It was left to Marianne to rescue them both from this awkward situation, which she did by the simple method of retiring to her room to supervise the remainder of her packing. The Earl was thus left conveniently alone and could receive his uncle's secretary without having to make any explanations or perform any embarrassing introductions.

The ornate jewel case, lavishly embossed with Florentine scrollwork, was strapped on to the back of his saddle, and the Earl, while feeling remarkably foolish, was unable to prevent himself from peering nervously around Berkeley Square, half anticipating the sight of a mysterious and sinister foreigner behind every lamp-post. It was in the midst of one such surreptitious survey that Marianne descended the steps of Rodbourne House, looking enchantingly self-possessed and elegant in a travelling pelisse of bronze wool with a matching bonnet trimmed by trailing white ostrich feathers. The Earl looked at Marianne in silence, not attempting to explain to himself why the entrancing picture presented by his wife merely served to deepen his ill-humour. He was acutely conscious of the fact that he had not emerged a victor from their small joust at the breakfast table, so he greeted her coolly.

"I shall ride Ebony," he said stiffly, patting his horse's neck. "I find travelling inside a carriage an intolerable bore and avoid it whenever possible."

Marianne greeted this arrangement with perfect equanimity. "Now I shall be able to stretch out and make myself really comfortable," she said, smiling innocently. "I find travelling so much pleasanter when one is not forced to make idle conversation." Her lashes swept down demurely to cover dark eyes, brimming with laughter. The Earl ground his teeth and wondered why such good sense and apparent willingness to please should render him so thoroughly disgruntled.

After a few hours of riding in the fresh air of an unseasonably warm and sunny October day, the Earl's temper was sufficiently recovered to enable him to examine his own feelings more calmly. He acknowledged, since he was an innately honest man, that his ill-humour sprang basically from regret at having accepted his uncle's mission. With a sudden start of surprise, he realized that he resented the intrusion of extraneous tasks into the delicate fabric of his marriage. In his astonishment at the train of his own thoughts, he pulled Ebony to a halt, staring back across the Kentish fields in the direction of the road still to be traversed by his wife's travelling carriage and the coach containing servants and household baggage. He wondered what Marianne was thinking, if she was as curious about her husband as he was about his wife.

The Earl savoured the feelings growing inside him with a sense of disbelief. He could never before remember experiencing this intense interest in a woman's mind and character while at the same time—he admitted it now—his desire to possess her body was increasing hourly.

He was seized by an irrational need to see Marianne again, to examine her face and see if in reality some flaw marred the perfection he remembered, to find—if he could—some traces of stupidity or greed that would blot out the frank and intelligent enticement of her eyes. Intensely violet eyes, he remembered, that seemed to be luring him on to a commitment he was far from ready to make.

Impatiently he touched his spurs to the flank of his horse, and the stallion leapt forward in obedience to the unspoken command. He was alongside the carriage within minutes, wheeling his horse around and trotting slowly as he glanced in the window of his wife's carriage.

Marianne lay back against the satin squabs, her hat discarded at her feet, brown curls tumbling in disorder around her shoulders. Her pelisse remained primly buttoned, her small shoes tucked discreetly under the hem of her travelling dress. The Earl stared at her long black lashes curling on to pale white cheeks and searched very hard for a blemish that would set him free from the invisible bonds he felt were tightening around him. He could find none. Once she was awake, he reassured himself, he would soon grow tired of her shrewish tongue.

The Tarrisbroke estate in Kent spread over more than two hundred acres of fertile land some twenty miles inland from the coastal port of Dover. The road between London and Tonbridge Wells was much frequented and maintained in a state of high repair, but the road later deteriorated and even with three changes of the horses drawing the carriages, it was not possible to accomplish the sixty miles from London to Tarrisbroke Hall in less than eight hours.

It was therefore almost evening when the Earl drew his horse, trembling with exhaustion, to a standstill outside the moss-encrusted pillars of the entrance to his home. His wife's travelling carriage, and the baggage coach, both provided with fresh horses at the last posting inn, drove briskly down the long gravelled driveway and came to a halt alongside the Earl.

Two grooms and a couple of stable boys ran swiftly round from the back of the house, and as soon as his horse was secured, the Earl swung to the ground and strode over to Marianne's carriage, gratefully easing cramped muscles that ached from hours in the saddle. Marianne appeared a little pale, but brushed aside his curt enquiry as to whether the swaying motion of the coach had affected her. With extreme formality, he offered her his arm to escort her into the house, but she stopped him and started to speak with unaccustomed embarrassment.

"I am afraid, my lord, that I have had no opportunity to become acquainted with the details of your family history. I should be obliged if you would tell me the names of those members of your family whom we are likely to be meeting this evening." She did not look directly at her husband. "I should not like to seem discourteous . . . or ill-educated . . . by making some muddle, or by overlooking some person to whom I owe attention."

The Earl was stricken with a novel feeling of remorse, which he overcame by speaking even more sharply than usual.

"Only my mother, the Dowager Countess, and my sister, Lady Eleanor, need concern you this evening. And since it is well known that I have been out of the country for many years, and the story has been put about that we met abroad, nobody will find it at all strange that you are singularly ignorant in all matters connected with my family and the disposition of my estates."

To his astonishment, Marianne laughed a little. "Indeed sir, I think this is one occasion when I may safely bless the fact of my feminine sex. I think I could probably live to be a hundred and no member of your acquaintance would find it in the least strange if I *still* knew nothing of the extent of your land, nor the general methods of administration you employ."

The Earl spoke with unthinking condescension. "I am quite sure that a lady blessed with such extraordinary good looks as your own, will not need to involve herself in the mundane problems of running a dairy herd!"

"Oh no!" said Marianne agreeably. "It is, after all, a well-acknowledged fact that a pretty face can only be retained if the brain is kept scrupulously empty of all useful knowledge." She smiled sweetly at the Earl, her manner guileless and disarming, yet he was once again left with the uncomfortable certainty that he had engaged in a sparring match and been defeated.

He was more than happy to feel the stirring of a sharp Autumn breeze, and wrapped a shawl around Marianne's shoulders with sudden solicitude. He carefully avoided the need for a reply by ushering her up the crumbling stone steps to the massive oak doors of Tarrisbroke Hall.

The butler, an old man of at least seventy, born on the estate and brought up to consider the Earls of Tarrisbroke as of considerably more consequence than the King and only slightly less consequence than the Almighty, bowed low as his master and new mistress entered the Great Hall. Although Harper could never have brought himself to form the thought, much less to express such a thought in words, he was inexpressibly relieved that the Old Earl had finally passed on and that the Young Earl had been able to come home before utter ruin visited the House of Rodbourne. Like all the other Tarrisbroke servants, Harper had not been paid for over a year, but he still bowed humbly as the Earl smiled at him, and he said with perfect sincerity, "Welcome home, my lord. It is an honour to see you and her ladyship.

As he spoke, Marianne stared about her in the silence of total incredulity. In her worst nightmares, she had never envisaged such a scene as this. On either side of the whole forty-foot length of the Great Hall, servants were lined up in neat and obviously expectant rows, females on the left-hand side, males on the right. From some source or another funds had been found to outfit the entire staff in black mourning liveries, and to Marianne the assembled ranks resembled nothing so much as rows of bats clustering in an abandoned building. With one corner of her panic-stricken brain she registered two awesome figures, one trailing voluminous, all-enveloping black veils, who stood at the very end of the Hall and thus constituted a physical barrier that had to be breached before the interior of the house could be attained.

With faint hope, she scanned the assembled ranks searching for Miss Thatcher's familiar and cheerful face. But there was no sign of her companion, and with a tiny sigh Marianne resigned herself to the fact that she would have to meet this challenge alone.

Marianne turned to face the Earl, for the first time a hint of real fear darkening her eyes, and to her great relief, his arm was placed firmly beneath her elbow, and his hand took her gloved fingers securely within his grasp. With complete assurance, he walked up to the elderly lady who headed the row of female servants lined up on the left of the Hall, and murmuring some polite words of recognition, told Marianne that this was Mrs. Withelmstone, the housekeeper. Swiftly he walked down the long lines of servants, nodding to some, shaking hands with others, smiling to them all.

Marianne smiled at the blur of faces until her jaws ached, while all the time she was thinking, "All these servants, and he was so desperate for money that he had to marry me!" Reluctantly, her exhausted brain decided that it could not unravel the mysteries of aristocratic systems of finance tonight.

Finally the never-ending litany of names came to a stop and Marianne found herself face-to-face with the two figures encased in black who stood at the end of the Hall. Instantly she became aware of the soft glow of her bronze pelisse, the quiver of her white ostrich plumes. Heavens, she thought desperately, was I supposed to be dressed like them?

The elder of the two figures inclined a regal head in Marianne's direction, and the Earl's grasp on her fingers increased perceptibly. "Mama," he said quietly, "I should like to present to you my wife, Marianne, Countess of Tarrisbroke."

"How do you do?" The imperious head bent fractionally, allowing Marianne to complete a suitably docile curtsy before a withered cheek, partially screened by scratchy lace veil, was placed against the soft firm skin of Marianne's face.

The second black figure, lacking the embellishment of lace veils, was more readily recognizable as a young woman of pleasing complexion, light blonde hair and rather pale grey eyes. These were turned upon Marianne without any noticeable warmth, and the Earl's accents were constrained as he made the second introduction. "Marianne, this is my sister, the Lady Eleanor."

Hesitantly, Marianne reached forward her hand, and when Lady Eleanor made no further gesture of greeting, she leant across the space separating them and touched her face against the unyielding surface of Lady Eleanor's cheek. "Lady Eleanor," she said with all the enthusiasm she could muster, "I am pleased to think that we are to be sisters. I am looking forward to arranging with you how we may most happily and usefully fill our days together at Tarrisbroke."

A momentary look of complacency crossed Lady Eleanor's features. "Since you have been brought up in Manchester, I am sure that there is a great deal I shall be able to teach you."

Marianne bit back an overhasty retort to the effect that she had not been brought up in Manchester, and had not precisely been asking her sister-in-law for instruction. She took a tight leash on her irritation and replied with commendable mildness, "I am not much used to country ways, having spent the last few years abroad. I'm sure many things will seem strange to me at first, and I shall be happy to have your advice."

Lady Eleanor seemed all set to enter into a dissertation upon the customs obtaining in Kent, but the Earl interrupted smoothly. "I am sure, Mama, that you will wish to serve dinner at the usual hour. Therefore you must excuse us if we are to dress ourselves more suitably before six o'clock. Perhaps Mrs. Withelmstone could show my wife to her rooms? I do not know which suite has been prepared for her."

There was a slight pause, full of tension, and Marianne suddenly became aware of the surprising fact that the relationship between her husband and his family was far from perfect. She had not previously spared the time from her own worries to wonder much about the feelings of the Earl towards his family, but now she could sense the coldness that resulted from long years of separation and the long-standing animosity between the Earl and his father.

She instinctively sympathized with the Dowager's reluctance to hand over the reins of domestic power, and so she tried to make some suggestion that would show her indifference as to the choice of bedchamber, but the Dowager was already speaking in a cold voice that prohibited interruptions.

"The master suites in the East Wing have been prepared for you," she said with careful neutrality. "We are a small, informal party this evening, so you need not make a very elaborate *toilette*." Almost as an afterthought she said to Marianne, "Your companion, Miss Thatcher, arrived three or four hours ago. She is resting in her room now."

"Why, that is splendid!" said Marianne happily. "I am so glad that Miss Thatcher was able to arrive here promptly. I should *like* to go and seek her out immediately, but you need not worry, ma'am. I shall exercise great restraint and refrain from gossiping with her before dinner. I am well used to travelling and have learned not to delay unnecessarily over my dressing."

The friendly smile froze on her lips as the Dowager Countess observed her with hostile eyes. "Indeed?" said the Dowager finally. "How commendable."

A faint flush of anger coloured Marianne's cheeks, but she made no further comment, her attention caught by the reassuring pressure that spread along her arm as the Earl tightened his clasp upon her fingers. "I shall look forward to this evening's dinner, Mama," said the Earl. "It is fortunate that you and my wife will have this brief opportunity to make one another's acquaintance, since our plans for the immediate future have been unexpectedly changed."

The Dowager spoke sharply. "You are not planning to leave Tarrisbroke before the estates have been returned to some sort of order, I hope?"

The Earl smiled easily at his mother, and only Marianne noticed the faint tightening of the muscles along his jaw.

"Your feminine intuition has found us out," he said laconically. "We have decided, despite the warmth of your welcome to us, that we should accept Sir Henry Lane's invitation to join him in Brussels for a short while. We leave at the beginning of the week." He ignored the disapproval clouding his mother's aristocratic forehead, bowed with charming courtesy to his sister and then to the Dowager. "You will understand our need to retire immediately. Come, Lady Tarrisbroke. Allow me to show you to your rooms."

The vast hall in which the Tarrisbroke family assembled their guests prior to dining constituted an impressive memorial to the splendours and discomforts of an earlier age. Most of Tarrisbroke Hall had been subjected to intermittent attempts at modernization and "improvement", but in this one room the stonework of the ancient castle remained unaltered through five centuries of architectural renovation.

The beamed ceiling rose to a lofty eighteen foot peak, in a style vaguely reminiscent of the main aisle in a large cathedral, and the granite walls, decorated at the bottom with exquisitely carved linenfold panelling, soared grey and unadorned as they approached the roof. At some stage in the remote past, the floor had been covered with oaken planks of assorted sizes and these now cast pitfalls for the unwary in the shape of slopes and hummocks artfully concealed by a variety of threadbare rugs.

The fireplace, presumably intended for roasting oxen, filled half of one massive wall, and the small tree-trunk burning in the centre of the grate achieved a creditable standard in warming the chimneystack, although it unfortunately had little effect upon the arctic temperatures that prevailed in the room at large.

Miscellaneous oak chairs and suits of armour lined the walls, most of them probably in the places that had been assigned to them three or four hundred years before. Red velvet draperies, faded and sadly darned, hung over the narrow windows and billowed gently in the gusts of wind that entered through a plentiful supply of cracks in the lead panes.

Marianne turned to the fireplace, walking quickly towards the comforting glow of orange and yellow flame that at least held out the illusion of warmth. The groups of people seated around the fire stopped all conversation and waited with awe-inspiring politeness for her arrival in their midst. She was greatly heartened to see Miss Thatcher, looking as friendly and full of commonsense as ever, seated at one side of the group. She was even more relieved when the Earl rose languidly from his seat on the oaken settle and came forward to greet her, smiling in a way that set her pulses racing. "I see that you were not exaggerating your skills as the mistress of swiftly-made *toilettes*. Come, let me make some of our neighbours known to you. I had warned them we should have to wait another half-hour at least."

Marianne spoke quickly in an effort to conquer her nervousness. "The Rajah in Ranjipur liked to show his authority over the British traders by summoning us to his presence without warning. Miss Thatcher and I both learned how to change swiftly, for we discovered that he beat the litter-bearers if we did not return to his Palace within an hour of the original summons. Monstrous, was it not?"

"Intolerable." For a moment the Earl's attention was caught, and he forgot that introductions had not yet been made. "Was he a terrible man?"

"On the contrary, I found him charming and invariably courteous to Mr. Johnson and myself when we were in his presence. Of course, it was impossible to believe any of the promises that he made, or any of the commitments concerning trade that he gave to my husband. But I noticed that he was scrupulous in fulfilling any *social* obligations he had agreed upon."

"So very strange to find oneself in such barbarous surroundings," said Lady Eleanor with a slight shudder. "One feels the call of Christian duty to minister to such savages, of course. But the contamination of a constant heathen presence must eventually destroy the delicacy of spirit so essential to any lady of refinement."

"I do not believe that it is strictly accurate to refer to the natives of India as savage," murmured Marianne, but she was saved from further discussion by the intervention of her husband, who called her attention to a complacent young man, warming his coattails in front of the massive fireplace.

"Marianne, this is Mr. George Davenport our near neighbour and an old friend of the family. His land straddles ours both to the West and to the North."

Marianne exchanged punctilious greetings, and tried to force her tired brain to take in the names of the dozen or so guests that constituted the Dowager Countess's "small and informal" dinner party.

It was a true pleasure to slip into a chair beside Helen Thatcher and indulge in the commonplace exchange of enquiries about the journey from town and the Earl's changed plans for the immediate future. Miss Thatcher professed herself all eagerness to explore Brussels, and Marianne was relieved to have assured herself of the presence of such a genial companion.

Conscious of her duties as the new Countess, however, Marianne spoke only briefly to Miss Thatcher before grimacing ruefully. "I suppose I must face this terrifying array of female tigers. . . . No doubt brought in by the Dowager especially to test my mettle. I am really surprised that she risked exposing herself to humiliation. After all, she had never met me and could not guess how I might behave."

Miss Thatcher glanced up at the Dowager and said

shrewdly, "She is of the type that is determined to make others uncomfortable, even if she ruins her own life in the process. No wonder your father-in-law took to the gaming tables." She caught herself up self-consciously. "I am sorry Marianne. You would probably prefer me to accustom myself to speaking less frankly now that . . . now that you are a Countess."

Marianne's eyes sparkled with mock rage. "Oh no, Helen! Not you too! At any moment you are going to start sounding like dear brother Thomas, and tell me how *impressive* it is to be the wife of an Earl! If *you* cannot speak frankly to me, then I am lost indeed."

Miss Thatcher laughed more naturally. "Well, it's probably just as well that I have your permission to be blunt, because I fear that after five years of outspokenness, it would be a little difficult to change my habits. But go now, Marianne. Never let the Dowager have just cause for hinting that I kept you from your duties."

The long day of travel had left Marianne more tired than she cared to admit, so that it was with considerable effort that she turned from a conversation with the local Squire and tried to focus her straying attention upon her other dinner companion. Mr. George Davenport, she discovered, had travelled, and now wished to share his experiences with a fellow voyager.

"My dear Countess . . ." he paused, and Marianne nodded attentively. "How edifying it is that we who have journeyed over so much of the earth's surface can still derive so much pleasure in the little happenings of our neighbourhood!

"Yes," said Marianne rather doubtfully. "But I have only been to India, you know." Since this seemed a less than adequate response she added, "I did not know that you had travelled so extensively."

"I have sailed in the wake of the great Sir Walter. I crossed the Atlantic and spent six months in Virginia, one of our former American Colonies, you know. Ah!" he sighed nostalgically. "When once the human spirit has tasted novelty, how quickly the familiar scene becomes a bore!"

Marianne's bewilderment grew as she endeavoured to respond to a remark that seemed in direct contradiction to the statement Mr. Davenport had himself made only minutes previously. The slight silence did not deter her companion, however, who proceeded to lecture her upon the habits of the American Indian with exhausting detail and great condescension. Marianne found his ponderous manners alternately wearisome and laughable, and wondered why the Dowager Countess tolerated his company with such obvious complaisance until Lady Eleanor's comments later enlightened her.

"I saw during dinner that Mr. Davenport was so kind as to share with you the benefit of his superior education and understanding," said Lady Eleanor to Marianne as the ladies sat quietly in the drawing-room awaiting the arrival of the gentlemen from the delights of the dining table. Her eyes dropped modestly to the embroidery that occupied her hands.

"As we are sisters, I feel that I may hint to you the way matters stand between Mr. Davenport and myself. Of course, nothing can be *official* whilst Mama and I remain so deep in mourning, but it makes me happy just to think of the elevated life we shall be able to lead together. Dear

Mr. Davenport's thoughts are always secured so firmly on a Higher Plane, it makes me quite humble just to listen to the workings of such an extraordinary mind."

"Extraordinary indeed!" said Marianne dryly, and looked up to greet the arrival of the gentlemen with a smile of such obvious pleasure that the Earl detached himself from the procession of guests and came over to join her.

"Sleepy?" he asked Marianne in a soft undertone.

"A little. I always find it more difficult to make new acquaintances than I feel I should."

The Earl smiled at her. "You probably strive too hard to make yourself generally agreeable. Long years of social experience have finally taught me that only the most boorish of guests and the most thoughtless of hosts is ever accounted a true success."

Marianne laughed a little wryly. "From your perspective, no doubt such advice is sound. I think the Dowager, your mother, might have just cause for resentment, however, if she found her daughter-in-law was not only tainted by a commercial background, but also deficient in her manners." She lifted brilliant eyes to the Earl. "I'm afraid that deliberate rudeness is yet another indulgence limited to the higher reaches of the aristocracy." She crinkled her nose humourously. "Never fear. I plan in this, as in all ways, to be a dutiful wife. I shall stand in front of my bedroom mirror and practice delivering insults in a suitably aristocratic manner."

"Lady Tarrisbroke . . . Marianne. . . ." The Earl's voice contained a note of new and disturbing urgency, but the rest of his words remained unspoken as the Dowager Countess, in the company of her daughter and Mr. Davenport, descended purposefully upon the couple.

"Well, sir," Mr. Davenport greeted the Earl jovially. "We have come to hear from the lips of your lovely Countess some of the excitements of her stay in India." He paused just long enough to beam at his audience, before turning to Marianne. "I understand that the native women of India are all in the habit of wearing a golden ring through their noses, which makes it easier for their husbands to lead 'em about, I'll be bound. Perhaps we should try and introduce the custom here!" And he laughed heartily at his own good joke.

"No," said Marianne baldly. "Indian women don't wear rings through their noses. You have confused the tribal customs of Africa with the ancient civilization of the Indian continent."

"Well!" cried Lady Eleanor in astonishment. "I think you must be mistaken, for Mr. Davenport has read *every* important book about India, and you may be sure he could not be in error."

"Of course not," said Marianne ironically. "I understand perfectly. How could the evidence of my own eyes count in the face of such prolific and careful study?"

Miss Thatcher tried unsuccessfully to smother a gasp of laughter, and while Lady Eleanor and Mr. Davenport smiled at each other complacently, the Earl spoke softly to Marianne.

"I do not think you require much practice in the arts we were just discussing. I feel the manners of the *haut ton* come easily to you!"

Marianne had the grace to blush, and attempted no further remonstrance with Mr. Davenport, feeling quite content to allow Lady Eleanor and her swain to re-organize the society of India to their own entire mutual satisfaction in a manner at variance with most of the known facts. In truth, the long journey and the strain of the past days were finally exerting their full effects, and it was only by the exercise of considerable will-power that she managed to nod and smile whenever Mr. Davenport paused for praise or approbation.

The Earl, who even without the benefit of a stay in India, was perfectly capable of judging Mr. Davenport's eloquence for what it was worth, watched Marianne's dropping eyelashes with an unexpected rush of tenderness. He waited for Mr. Davenport to draw a deep breath, before saying with ruthless finality, "Very true. Everything you say is marvellously perceptive."

He turned to the Dowager Countess, who was regarding her son with a slight, almost imperceptible, frown. "Mama," said the Earl, "Marianne is exhausted from our long journey. You will forgive us, I know, if I escort her to her room.

The Dowager spoke quietly. "I understand that the Countess, who is unused to gatherings such as this, may feel tired. However, my dear Quentin, there are several of our lady guests who have not yet had an opportunity to speak with you. I think we must ask the Countess to retire alone, so that *you* may fulfil the obligations of your position."

Marianne got quickly to her feet and looked directly at the Dowager. "I would not dream of detaining the Earl from his duties," she said stiffly. "I am quite capable of calling for my own maid." She nodded briefly to Lady Eleanor and to Mr. Davenport, before turning back to the

Dowager. "I must ask for your kindness, ma'am, in making my excuses to the remainder of your guests."

She walked swiftly to the heavy doors of the salon and swept through without a backward glance.

CHAPTER NINE

Once in the comfortable darkness of the upper hallways, her hot cheeks cooled by the icy blasts of October wind that whistled round the stone corridors, Marianne regained control of her temper. Now that her immediate anger was dissipated, she regretted her impetuous withdrawal from the drawing-room, not least because she soon found herself wandering aimlessly up and down the gloomy recesses of the hallway, searching for the carved and curtained doorway which led to her suite of rooms. Tarrisbroke Hall, if not quite the turreted castle her brother had dreamed of, was certainly large enough to permit virtually endless wandering about its dimly lit corridors.

Just as she was on the point of swallowing her pride and returning downstairs to request the assistance of Miss Thatcher or Lady Eleanor, she found herself facing the blue damask hangings which she remembered marked the entrance to her bedchamber. Sighing with relief, she thrust her hands under the dusty silk tassels, eyeing the grey smudges on her wrists with disfavour. Her sister-in-law, she thought uncharitably, would be better employed checking the activities of the chambermaids and ensuring that the upper footmen remained on duty in their appointed positions, rather than listening in perpetually open-mouthed wonder to the inanities of Mr. Davenport.

The door, lacking oil on its hinges as well as polish on its panels, finally swung open with a sudden burst of noise, and Marianne walked into the room, her hand reaching out automatically for the bell-rope to summon her maid.

The summons was never completed, however, for to her considerable embarrassment she found herself staring into the startled eyes of a soberly-dressed gentleman, not much older than herself. "I beg your pardon," said Marianne, anxious to explain the mistake which had caused her unwarranted intrusion. "I had thought this was my bedchamber. You must forgive me walking into your room. The hangings outside the door are identical with those outside my room."

The young man smiled politely, listening to her muddled outpouring with silent courtesy. As soon as she finished speaking he executed a low bow and murmured, "It is nothing, *Madame*," and with a gesture of his arm indicated that he would escort her to the door.

Marianne responded to the gesture, but as she turned to leave the room her glance happened to light upon the remarkable jewel-case that was partially obscured by the young man's body. She looked round the room with sudden suspicion, noting the monogrammed brushes laid out on a dressing table, and spying in one corner a familiar green riding coat.

"But this is my husband's room!" she exclaimed in surprise. She spoke impatiently to the young man, too tired and worried to eliminate the note of accusation that lingered in her voice. "Why are you in the Earl's bedchamber? You are not a servant."

"Your husband's room? For a moment, the young man

seemed at a loss for words, then astonishment was once more replaced by bland courtesy.

He bowed again, more gracefully than ever. "A thousand apologies for disturbing you, my lady. I am an old friend of the Earl and he wrote asking me to wait for him here, in his own rooms. I may be an old friend but. . . ." He allowed his shoulders to lift expressively. "I regret to have to admit it, I am not one who finds favour with the Countess of Tarrisbroke." He corrected himself swiftly, flashing Marianne an altogether charming smile. "I should say, my lady, with the *Dowager* Countess of Tarrisbroke."

"I see," said Marianne thoughtfully. The young man's foreign accent was not pronounced, but she had no difficulty in discerning the hint of some European inflection behind the carefully chosen words. She had no difficulty, either, in believing that the Earl's friends would find little favour with the formidable Dowager. Her own experiences during the evening predisposed her to feel charitable towards all those individuals who had fallen foul of the Dowager's cold notions of hospitality, but—despite the plausibility of the young man's story, a lingering suspicion hovered at the edges of her mind. She tried to convince herself that she did not know the Earl well enough to judge how he might treat his friends. Moreover she was only too ready to acknowledge that the code of manners existing between gentlemen was quite incomprehensible to her. Nevertheless, she could not believe that the Earl would leave an old friend lurking in his bedchamber while he beguiled his time at a family dinner party.

As if reading her thoughts, the young man crossed to her side and said easily, "I have spent many nights waiting for

Lord Rodbourne ... the Earl ... to join me, my lady. You need not fear that either he or I find such an arrangement at all strange." His dark eyes flashed impudently. "I fear that our meeting tonight must be something in the nature of a farewell. I cannot believe that my good friend will be spending many more evenings away from his own home!"

Marianne decided to give up the struggle to intervene in her husband's personal affairs. "I trust the Earl will not keep you waiting long," she said stiffly. "I will bid you goodnight."

As soon as she was outside the door of the Earl's bedroom, she could see her own room at the other side of the alcove, the entrance marked with identically dusty blue draperies. Becky, her abigail, waited patiently in the spacious dressing-room, and Marianne was happy to allow the maid to undress her in a companionable silence. It was soothing to take refuge in the familiar routine of bedtime, and to let Becky's capable hands ease the brush through her hair, smoothing away the tensions of an exhausting day.

How could she have imagined five weeks ago that her life would take on such a sudden and startling change? She felt a sudden irresistible urge to giggle as she stared round at the faded splendours of her bedchamber and contrasted it with the cheerfully vulgar opulence of her brother's townhouse. She resolutely ignored the small part of her heart that insisted upon pointing out that she actually felt more at home amid the draughty grey stones of Tarrisbroke than the comfortable modern brick of the Perkins' townhouse.

But all impulse towards solitary mirth vanished as they heard the sounds of approaching footsteps, followed by the sharp voice of the Dowager and the firm, cool tones of the

Earl as he bade his mother a polite goodnight.

Marianne's body stiffened with an involuntary movement, and she tried to avoid meeting Becky's eyes in the mirror, not wanting to see there any awareness of the nervous tension that tautened her responses. There was no knock on the door, however, and the maid ventured no remark of a personal nature. She walked over to the lamps lodged high on the mantelpiece, extinguishing some candles as she passed by. "Do you wish me to leave the lamps, my lady?" she asked quietly.

"Yes," said Marianne, and then thought again. "Er . . . no. I have had a long day, I think I shall sleep immediately."

"As you wish, my lady. Good night."

The door opened with an inevitable creak and was shut quietly behind the maid.

Darkness descended upon the room and Marianne stirred restlessly in the great bed, free at last to give rein to her chaotic thoughts. She tossed on the soft down pillows for over an hour before her natural honesty forced her to admit that she was not really staying awake in order to find solutions for the day's problems, and that since the Earl seemed to have no intention of entering his wife's bedroom, she might as well compose herself for sleep.

She pounded the pillows with unladylike vigour and resolutely prepared herself for sleep.

The morning sunshine inspired Marianne to view the world with fresh optimism. Whatever the problems of her marriage, Tarrisbroke Hall was clearly in need of a firm hand in charge of the housekeeping. Since neither the Dowager nor Lady Eleanor appeared to take any interest in the management of trivial domestic affairs, Marianne decided to spend the few days prior to their departure for Belgium engaged in the servants' quarters.

While it might be tactless to sweep through the house pouring out money on new window hangings and wall coverings, surely in her own rooms she might, with perfect propriety, introduce some new furnishings and change the colour scheme from faded grey to fresh yellow.

Cheered by these pleasantly familiar prospects of domestic management, Marianne ventured downstairs defiantly robed in a morning gown of dusky pink that could only by the exercise of the greatest charity be considered matronly.

Lady Eleanor greeted her at the breakfast table with smiling condescension, apologising for her mother's absence. The Dowager, it seemed, had already eaten and left to pursue whatever activities she considered appropriate to her station. Marianne squashed a small flicker of disappointment when she saw no sign of her husband, and wished that pride did not prevent her asking for information from Lady Eleanor. She would have to pin her hopes on Miss Thatcher, who had greeted Marianne with a cheery smile, ignored Lady Eleanor's barbed politeness, and who now continued her phlegmatic consumption of toast and honey.

By exercising considerable tact and allowing herself to be instructed on whatever subject Lady Eleanor introduced into the conversation, breakfast was brushed through without any unpleasantness, Lady Eleanor so far unbending as to suggest that Mrs. Withelmstone might be called for in order to show Marianne something of the routines of the household. Marianne accepted the suggestion gratefully, pleased that it had come unbidden from her sister-in-law, and they parted on a note of amity Marianne could hardly have anticipated the previous evening. She only hoped that poor Miss Thatcher, born off to inspect Lady Eleanor's collection of water-colours, was equally reconciled to the morning's arrangements.

Mrs. Withelmstone, the housekeeper, conducted Marianne through the main rooms with a defensive attitude bordering upon hostility. And in truth, Marianne thought wryly, she had much to be defensive about. The sheen of neglect was everywhere, from the unbrushed rugs to the undusted corners, to the dull mirrors and the cobwebs festooning the high ceilings. Marianne bit her tongue to hold back the unfavourable comments, waiting for Mrs. Withelmstone to finish the sad little tour.

The end of the inspection came more quickly than Marianne anticipated. The housekeeper conducted her new mistress out of the family portrait gallery, a long gloomy room, full of unrealistically dignified Earls staring out of tarnished gilt frames, and waited with hands folded for Marianne's comments.

Marianne smiled with more friendliness than she felt, and asked if she might see the kitchens.

"The kitchens, my lady?" Mrs. Withelmstone's expression struggled between incredulity and a touch of awe. "You wish to look in the kitchens, my lady?"

"Yes," said Marianne patiently. "I cannot tell how we could make your tasks easier if I have not inspected the kitchens. And when the Earl and I return from our stay in Brussels, I shall wish you to take me into all the main bedrooms, and the servants' quarters as well." She smiled kindly. "I can only find out where new linen and furnishings are needed if I have seen all the main rooms."

"Oh my lady! Madam. . . ." To Marianne's horror, Mrs. Withelmstone's rigid face crinkled suspiciously at the corner of her eyes, and the housekeeper gave every indication that she might at any moment burst into tears. But after a slight struggle and several sniffs, she regained control and rushed into apologies. "My lady, you can't come into the kitchens today," she said agitatedly. "The roaches is running around the floor something terrible this morning and the pots not scoured since last night's dinner. Only give me till tomorrow, to make it more suitable for your ladyship."

Marianne found herself torn between amusement and disgust. "You may have heard that I have lived in India," she told the housekeeper. "So I'm quite sure that I have seen cockroaches and other insects larger than any you could even dream of. However, Mrs. Withelmstone, I must ask you why the kitchens are in such a state of disarray? Surely it should be possible to scour the pans immediately after a meal and thus avoid attracting rats, mice and all the other unpleasant inhabitants who are undoubtedly sharing Tarrisbroke Hall with us?"

"Well, of course," said Mrs. Withelmstone matter-of-factly. "But there's a limit to what two skivvies and a potboy can do, all on their own."

Marianne was puzzled. "Mrs. Withelmstone, I am not yet familiar with the numbers of servants employed by the estate. But I am quite sure that yesterday I was introduced to at least twenty female servants and a corresponding number of males. Why can they not be persuaded to perform their appointed functions?"

The housekeeper looked at Marianne consideringly before speaking. "It's true that there are sixteen womenfolk working inside the Hall, my lady. But two of the girls you met yesterday are lady's maids to the Dowager and the Lady Eleanor, so they won't turn a hand when it comes to housework. Two of the girls assist the chef. Then there's a girl working in the stillroom, two working on the sewing, there's the laundry maids, and the girls we need to clean all the bedchambers. Many's the day I hardly know where to turn to get all the work done."

"Well," said Marianne briskly, "we must hire sufficient people to make Tarrisbroke Hall perfectly habitable again, and then once everything is in good order we may consider if more servants are required permanently. With winter coming on, I'm sure many of the village labourers would be glad of some extra work."

The housekeeper said only, "Yes, my lady. Thank you, my lady," but the look of unspeakable gratitude that flashed into her eyes convinced Marianne that the Hall's sad air of neglect was not attributable to Mrs. Withelmstone's lack of interest. "I shall leave the hiring of extra servants in your hands, Mrs. Withelmstone. And perhaps you could recommend a local tradesman who would help me to make some changes in the decoration of my rooms? I have been used to rather . . . brighter colours."

The housekeeper's response to Marianne's decorative plans was never revealed, however, for their solitary seclusion near the gallery was interrupted by the portly figure of the butler, whose coughing and nervous foot-shuffling Marianne correctly interpreted as an urgent desire to speak with her privately. She searched her memory and triumphantly came up with his name. "Yes, Harper," she said. "Do you wish to say something to me?" She smiled at the housekeeper and murmured, "I must not keep you from your duties, Mrs. Withelmstone," forcing the housekeeper to retire with as good grace as she could muster.

The butler scarcely waited for the housekeeper's crackling black skirts to swish round the corner of the hallway, before he bowed yet again to Marianne and asked if she could be so good as to tell him exactly where the Earl might be found.

"I have not seen my husband this morning," said Marianne with outward tranquillity. "Is there some special reason why you need him?"

The butler seemed loathe to speak, and staring intently at his feet could be heard to mutter something to the effect that it was, after all, scarcely past noon. Marianne, who felt that the servants of Tarrisbroke Hall were displaying idiosyncratic characteristics almost as startling as their masters, spoke with more sharpness than usual. "If you have no further questions, Harper, I think I should like to see something of the gardens."

The butler evidently reached a decision swiftly, for he ceased examining his toes and brought his eyes up to face Marianne. "It's the master," he said simply. "His valet has been waiting this two hours and more for a call to the Earl's room. And when nobody heard anything, Smith went into the room to check on the master personally. The bells in the house aren't all that we should wish, my lady, and Smith didn't like to think of his lordship hanging about fuming for his hot water."

The butler paused to consider the effect his tale was having upon the Countess, but finding himself unable to discern any particular expression on her perfectly formed features, he reluctantly brought himself to the point of his story. "The Earl wasn't in his rooms, my lady." He coughed delicately. "The bed had not been touched, my lady, and Smith says that . . . er . . . that his lordship has gone out wearing his evening clothes from last night." The butler sighed. "And now the bailiff is here, my lady, and he is waiting to talk to his lordship. The bailiff says that his lordship sent word down from Town ordering him to meet the Earl this morning. And now the Earl isn't here, my lady and nobody seems to know where he has gone."

The continued immobility of Marianne's features allowed no hint of her tumultuous inner feelings to show upon her face. She spoke to the butler with careful calm. "I believe my husband's valet has been with him for many years?"

"Yes, my lady," replied the butler, relieved that he seemed to be brushing through such a delicate encounter with his new mistress without serious embarrassment. "Smith has been with his lordship ever since his lordship's sixteenth birthday. He stayed with the Earl all the time, even when his lordship was living in Italy and places like that." Remembering too late that the Countess was reputed to have spent several years abroad, he added dutifully, "I expect foreign parts is very agreeable once you're used to them."

Marianne ignored this evidence of the butler's nationalistic tendencies and spoke with sudden decision. "Offer the bailiff some refreshment, Harper, and convey the Earl's apologies. You may say that we shall send for him again as soon as possible." She smiled at the butler, unconsciously utilizing the natural charm of manner that had made the Johnson home the only efficiently-run household in Ranjipur. "Perhaps you would also be good enough to ask the Dowager Countess and the Lady Eleanor if they have seen the Earl this morning? I know I can rely upon you not to alarm them with any hint that the Earl's whereabouts may be . . . generally unknown."

She walked quickly to the foot of the great staircase. "I shall be waiting in my own sitting-room. Would you tell Smith to come to me there immediately?"

"Yes, my lady." The butler allowed his shoulders to sag with relief that all decision-taking had been removed from his area of responsibility. Happily he walked off, the tails of his livery flapping against the back of his legs in dignified rhythm.

Marianne sighed as she climbed up the stairs, paying no heed to her surroundings until she reached the alcove that marked the entrance to the two master suites. There she stopped and frowned at the two sets of blue draperies in sudden remembrance. Wryly she allowed the significance of her conversation with the butler to push to the surface of her thoughts. The Earl of Tarrisbroke was missing from his home after two days of marriage, and the Countess of Tarrisbroke had no idea where he had gone.

Marianne entered her room, freshly cleaned by Mrs. Withelmstone's own hands, but the sparkling windows and gleaming furniture gave her no pleasure. She sat on the edge of a chaise longue, newly provided with small soft pillows, and nibled thoughtfully at the end of one finger. The mantle of the Countess of Tarrisbroke, she decided, did not yet sit very comfortably on the shapely shoulders of Marianne Johnson, widow, daughter of Thomas Perkins, cloth merchant.

CHAPTER TEN

Timothy Smith knocked decorously on the Countess of Tarrisbroke's private door, and waited for her permission to enter. His years of travel on the Continent of Europe appeared to have left little mark upon his face and figure. From the top of his smooth brown hair, through every detail of his sober black uniform, right down to the tips of his polished leather slippers, he proclaimed his status as gentleman's gentleman to a member of the British aristocracy. Not for him the affectations of his inferior counterparts in France and Italy. He was happy to establish his professional excellence by the superior cut of his handsome black jacket and the fine quality of his linen shirt.

Marianne examined the studiously correct bearing of the valet with some wariness. Her unexpected success with the housekeeper and the butler did not lead her into any false expectations that good relations with her husband's valet would be similarly easy to establish. He, above all people, must be perfectly well aware that her acquaintance with the Earl was of the briefest and most formal nature.

"Harper tells me that neither the Dowager Countess nor the Lady Eleanor has any idea where the Earl might have gone," said Marianne eventually. She looked frankly at the valet. "I have no ideas either, Smith, and I hope that you will be able to help us."

The valet failed to relax his guard. "His lordship did not call for my services last night, my lady. So I would not care to venture a suggestion as to where his lordship may have gone."

"The Earl made an appointment to see his bailiff this morning and he has failed to keep that appointment." Marianne waited a few moments and then added mildly, "I would not have thought that the Earl was either forgetful or inconsiderate where his family and servants are concerned."

"Oh no, my lady!" The valet looked distressed. "It *is* strange that his lordship didn't tell anybody where he was going."

"Was it you, Smith, who admitted the Earl's friend to his chambers last night?"

The atmosphere of bristling wariness immediately returned, and the valet said doubtfully, "A friend, my lady?"

"Yes." Mariane could scarcely control her impatience. "A young man, slim, medium height, with dark curly hair. He speaks with just the slightest of foreign accents. His complexion was somewhat tanned, as if he had been travelling considerable distances on horseback."

"A gentleman!" The startled exclamation broke out before Smith could contain his surprise, and Marianne felt a twitch of chagrin when she realized that the valet had feared the presence of a female "friend" in the Earl's bedroom. "The Earl never mentioned no visitors to me last night, my lady. And I can't imagine as how he'd have visitors waiting on him in his bedchamber. It's not like when we was forced to accommodate ourselves in rooms.

Here we have the whole Hall at our disposal. Why should we receive gentlemen in our bedchamber?"

Marianne was amused to see that the valet, at least, retained a very proper sense of the dignity befitting an Earl. She hesitated for just a moment before deciding upon a policy of complete honesty with a servant whose loyalty was almost certainly beyond question.

"But however strange it may seem, Smith, the gentleman I have described was quite definitely in my husband's room, because I saw him there. He told me that he was an old friend of the Earl and that he had been asked to wait in the Earl's bedchamber because the Dowager Countess did not . . . does not. . . . In short, the Dowager Countess would not have been pleased to welcome this particular friend of the Earl to her drawing-room."

The valet's puzzlement appeared to grow. "But the Dowager don't know any of the Earl's foreign friends, my lady. When we came back to London in September it was the first time we was officially in England for ten years. Of course, the Earl has stopped off in London now and again and spent some time with one or two of his oldest cronies, but he never visited Tarrisbroke not once—not since he and the old Earl had that terrible turn-up." The valet stopped suddenly, aware of indiscretion. "Anyway, my lady, how could the Dowager disapprove of somebody she never set eyes upon?"

Marianne was severely tempted to reply, "Quite easily!" but bit back the retort and tried to turn the valet's attention to the appearance of the interloper. "Does my descripion bring nobody in particular to mind, Smith? If we could but identify the man perhaps we could trace him and discover the course of the Earl's movements yesterday night." Nervously she twisted the soft velvet ribons that trimmed the waistline of her gown. "I cannot believe that all is well. I'm afraid . . . I'm very much afraid. . . . If only I knew exactly what had been discussed with Sir Henry."

"Sir Henry!" Smith's exclamation was triumphant. "That'll be it, my lady. You'll have seen one of Sir Henry's secretaries. He's always got half-a-dozen of these foreigners working around his office. Liaison officers, they're called, and they all look alike. Dark and foreign-looking, but speaking English so that you hardly know they aren't born and bred to it."

Relief flooded Marianne's body. She had not known how frightened she had been until Smith's explanation removed the need for concern. "Of course!" she said. "And the Dowager Countess could easily have made the acquaintance of one of Sir Henry's secretaries. Sir Henry is, after all, her brother."

"Yes." Suddenly the valet's voice reflected a fresh note of uncertainty. "But it's still queer that the Earl didn't leave any word of where he was going."

"Oh no!" Marianne refused to admit the dark note of doubt into her thoughts. "He will return to us shortly with some very simple explanation and we shall be left wondering why we did not think of it for ourselves." Briskly she rose to her feet. "Thank you, Smith, for the help you have given me in unravelling this little mystery. And now I am going to attempt to find the Lady Eleanor so that she may show me some of the delightful gardens I have been looking at from this window."

The valet stood still for a moment longer than was

proper in a perfectly trained servant. Then he bowed slowly, accepting his dismissal. "I am happy to be of assistance, my lady." He hesitated, with his hand poised above the door-knob. "I shall be in my quarters if you by any chance wish to send for me, my lady."

Marianne smiled gaily. "I'm sure his lordship will be asking you to bring him shaving water long before I am ever informed of his return!" she said.

"That could be, my lady," said the valet, and allowed the faintest hint of disapproval to stiffen the outline of his retreating back.

"It is really most inconsiderate of Quentin," said Lady Eleanor waspishly, as she helped herself to a generous portion of cold veal. "Of course, I would not venture to question the Earl's behaviour in a general way. But while we are *en famille* so to speak. . . ." Here she broke off to flash a coy simper in the direction of Mr. George Davenport, who was consenting to come down from his Higher Plane sufficiently to put away generous helpings of everything the luncheon table offered.

Mr. Davenport smiled kindly at Lady Eleanor and told her that nobody could possibly construe such sisterly remarks as criticism, which obvious untruth Lady Eleanor accepted with a grateful blush of pleasure. The Dowager Countess, who had been contemplating a portrait of her late husband that surmounted the dining-room mantelpiece with every appearance of true melancholy, remarked in sepulchral accents that she hoped her son was not about to bring fresh scandal upon the beleaguered house of Tarrisbroke.

Marianne could contain herself no longer. "Fresh scandal?" she asked. "I was not aware that the *present* Earl had achieved any degree of notoriety."

The Dowager looked at Marianne austerely. "My son's behaviour cannot suitably be discussed in the presence of two delicately bred and unmarried females." She allowed her eyes to slide over Miss Thatcher. "Not even one who has resided among heathens. Suffice to say that his behaviour on the Continent frequently caused his father and myself grave heartache."

Miss Thatcher resolutely avoided Marianne's gaze; Lady Eleanor cast her eyes modestly to her plate; Mr. Davenport looked solemn and Marianne stared around the table in open disbelief. "But there are only two possible explanations of the Earl's absence, and neither is very scandalous," she exclaimed. "Either he has received an urgent summons from his uncle, Sir Henry Lane, or he has met with some accident. It is impossible to see how either of those two eventualities could tarnish the reputation of the Rodbourne family—whatever youthful indiscretions my husband may have committed during his years of exile."

Lady Eleanor looked quite kindly at her sister-in-law. "But your husband resided abroad at his own wish," she said sadly. "Mama and I often wished he would come home and turn his mind from the frivolous pursuits that I am afraid occupied so *much* of his attention."

Marianne gave up. "Yes," she said. "I am aware that his exile from Tarrisbroke Hall was self-imposed." She turned to the Dowager. "Have you no apprehension that some . . . misadventure . . . may have befallen your son, ma'am? I confess that I am beginning to grow a little uneasy."

"No accident which involved an Earl of Tarrisbroke could occur without my knowing of it," said the Dowager placidly. She spoke repressively. "There are other reasons why a gentleman may decide to absent himself from his home."

Marianne's sympathy for the late earl increased another small notch, and compassion for her husband blossomed into full flower. How miserable his youth must have been, sandwiched between an icy mother, a simpering sister and an uncaring and spendthrift father. Small wonder that he regarded the world through a thick layer of protective cynicism.

Miss Thatcher hastened to introduce a less controversial topic and hit upon the excellent notion of questioning Mr. Davenport concerning the religious observances of the natives in Virginia. The meal continued under the flow of a virtual monologue from Mr. Davenport, ably spurred on by Miss Thatcher on the rare occasions when he showed dangerous signs of flagging.

The Dowager and her daughter finished eating and rose in perfect unison from the table. As the party of ladies made a stately exit from the room, Mr. Davenport bowed slightly to Miss Thatcher and drew Marianne to his side. "If I may steal your friend from you for just a moment, Miss Thatcher," he said.

He waited until the door closed safely behind the ladies before speaking to Marianne. "I feel sure, my dear Countess, that I may speak frankly to you, in a way that I could not in front of one who has been as delicately nurtured as the Lady Eleanor. If I may just drop a *hint* in your ear, I would like to suggest that you do not enquire too closely into the Earl's activities. Sometimes a wife must learn to be a little blind, you know."

Marianne replied coldly. "If you are suggesting, Mr. Davenport, that the Earl has chosen the third day of our marriage and his first day back in Tarrisbroke to pursue some illicit love affair, then I think I shall need to become more than a little blind if I am to endure our marriage. You cannot truly believe that the Earl's sense of responsibility is so far lacking that he could even contemplate such a gross neglect of his obligations."

"No, no! I intended no discourtesy. How could you think it of me." Mr. Davenport's head nodded in agitation. "It is only that the Earl's dislike of matrimony is so well known, and his—er—amatory adventures so much spoken of. I wish, dear lady, to spare you unnecessary pain." A few deep breaths served to restore his normal air of self-consequence. "We are all sensitive to the fact that your previous circumstances . . . that you are not . . . that you cannot be accustomed to *our* way of living."

Marianne forced herself to remember that Mr. Davenport's intentions were kind, and she placed a cool hand on his arm. "I think that I understand the Earl quite well, Mr. Davenport. Now I must take my leave of you, for I have to confer with some members of the household staff."

Mr. Davenport was for once quite relieved to find his conversation at an end. "Well, well. I shall not detain you," he said, making no move to leave Marianne's side. "Lady Eleanor is expecting me to escort her to the Vicarage this afternoon. Mrs. Chalmers and Lady Eleanor derive much pleasure in one another's company and I, of course, am always happy to bring my wide knowledge of the world to bear upon any little subject that may be troubling the Vicar." He tried to look modest and failed lamentably. "Sometimes I feel that the Vicar's sermons are almost as much my work as they are his. It's a fortunate gift, this knack that I have of being ever ready with the *mot juste*."

"It must be indeed," said Marianne. "And in my case, I think that the *mot juste* at this moment is undoubtedly goodbye."

"That is very good!" Mr. Davenport laughed heartily. "I see that the Earl has brought wit as well as beauty into the Rodbourne family."

Marianne effected her escape while Mr. Davenport still chuckled quietly to himself. With a contrariness of spirit that her brother would have recognized only too well, the determination of her new family to pass off the Earl's absence as an unfortunate piece of irresponsibility merely confirmed Marianne's nebulous suspicions that all was far from well with her husband.

She decided to seek out Miss Thatcher and discuss the situation with her old companion, and she went upstairs intending to find Miss Thatcher's bedchamber. But without consciously planning it, Marianne found herself waiting once more outside the door of her husband's rooms, and even as she stood wondering whether or not to enter, Smith appeared at the end of the corridor, approaching her with a gait as nearly resembling a run as his sense of dignity would permit.

"My lady!" He started to address her long before he reached her side. "My lady! There is a person outside who says he has a message from the Earl. He insists that he will deliver it only to you. Please come, my lady."

"But of course." Marianne was already following behind the valet, not bothering to ask if he suspected bad news. Everything about his agitated demeanour suggested great anxiety. She gathered up her skirts and quickened her steps to catch up with Smith's impatient progress along the upper hallway.

CHAPTER ELEVEN

The valet led the way down a small back staircase, coming to a halt in a dimly lighted room that led off the main kitchen. The room had probably once been used as the housekeeper's office, for it contained a somewhat rickety desk and chair, some old account books, and shelves bearing several dozen empty spice bottles. The muted sounds of iron ladles banging against pewter pots and the bustling chatter of young serving girls in the nearby kitchens, emphasized the stillness of this room and the immobility of the man who awaited Marianne's arrival.

He was of medium height, wearing a brown cloth coat of indeterminate fashion, and dusty shoes and breeches suggestive of a hard ride. His hands, incongruously white and long-fingered, toyed with a folded sheet of paper that he made no immediate move to pass to the Countess. She found his appraising stare disconcerting, and felt bewildered by the touch of insolence that lurked, indefinably present, behind the outward subservience of his bearing. She did not allow herself many seconds of silent scrutiny, however, since the need to have news of her husband far outweighed all other feelings.

"You have brought me a message from the Earl?" she asked abruptly. "I am the Countess of Tarrisbroke."

The man looked at her with a touch of mockery. "And I, *Madame*, am the *Baron* de Bellevigne. Your husband's letter is here."

Marianne reached out eagerly. "He is well? We began to fear some mishap had occurred." For the moment she did not bother to question why a French aristocrat should bring letters from her husband.

Gently the *Baron* removed the piece of paper from her reach, and looked pointedly in the direction of the valet, who remained in the room as a silent observer. "I think we could pursue this discussion more profitably if we were alone," said the *Baron*.

"But what has happened to my husband?" cried Marianne, fighting an upsurge of panic. The respectful obsequiousness of the *Baron* de Bellevigne suddenly seemed no guarantee of the Earl's safety, and she needed the reassurance of the valet's presence. "Smith is an old and trusted servant," she said. "There can be no reason for requesting his removal."

The *Baron* shrugged his shoulders impatiently. "No reason for you, perhaps, but several for me."

The valet moved forward and stood beside Marianne with a hint of aggression stiffening his manner. "Of course I shall stay if you need me, my lady."

"No, no." Marianne could brook no further delay in learning the contents of her husband's letter. "If you will wait for me in your quarters, Smith, I shall send for you as soon as *Monsieur le Baron* has left."

"Very well, my lady." Smith went from the bare room with evident reluctance, but Marianne spared him no more than one swift glance before turning back to the *Baron*. "I should be grateful if you would now hand over to me the message my husband has entrusted to you."

The *Baron* de Bellevigne bowed with mild irony. "You and your noble husband each share an equal impatience for news of the other, my lady." He handed Marianne the folded paper. "You will see that the Earl's message is brief. And to the point."

Marianne opened the letter with hands that shook slightly, despite her best efforts to control them. Her eyes rushed over the brief message.

"Please go with Bellevigne. Tarrisbroke."

The half dozen words quavered across the page in a shaky slope, halting at the signature with a dramatic and unattractive splotch of reddish-brown. White-cheeked, Marianne looked up at the *Baron*. "He is wounded? Where is he? Why can he not come back to the Hall? Is he too ill to move?"

The *Baron* de Bellevigne regarded her in speculative and nerve-wracking silence, then shrugged delicately. "His condition, my lady, could be much improved if you would but hand over to me the Crown of the Martyr that should have been contained in the jewelcase my ... associate ... removed from the Earl's bedroom last night."

"The Crown?" Marianne's voice hovered between impatience and mystification, and then as she gathered her scattered wits she whirled round accusingly. "Then the young man I saw last night *was* a burglar! I doubted all along that he could be a friend of the Earl's!"

"Come, come, my lady." The *Baron* made no effort to conceal his mounting irritation. "This pretence of ignorance is very affecting, but will cut no ice with me. Let us save ourselves a great deal of wasted time and effort and be honest with one another. You wish for the safe return of your husband. I wish for the Crown of the Martyr Saint Helen-Theodora. I know the whereabouts of the Earl. You know the whereabouts of the Crown. Let us effect an exchange of information at once, so that we both may be happy."

He smiled grimly. "The knowledge that in saving the Crown you delayed Prince Alberto's decision to transfer his loyalties away from the British Government will surely be of small consolation to you, should you find yourself again a widow so soon after becoming a wife."

He examined the dusty ruffles of his wrist band. "We know, my lady, that the Crown was delivered to Rodbourne House before you and the Earl left London, and my associate insists that it was not contained among the Earl's personal belongings. I must therefore assume, my lady, that your jewel case now houses a treasure that is almost beyond price."

"You are mad," said Marianne with conviction. "How can I convince you that I don't understand even one word of what you ask?" Her hands clutched involuntarily around the slim scrap of paper. "I beg that you will take me to the Earl, and I will ask him to give you this Crown. I can assure you that if it is some heirloom he has been saving, I will use my best efforts to persuade him that it can be of no importance in comparison with his own safety and wellbeing." Impulsively she reached out and touched his hands. "Please take me to the Earl. I must see him!"

The *Baron* de Bellevigne looked regretful. "My lady, I am afraid that time becomes pressing for all of us. I will no longer conceal from you the fact that the Earl requires the attentions of a surgeon, and I am sure you will not be surprised if I admit that the plans I have made with some of my fellow Frenchmen are now rushing towards a conclusion. To be brief, *madame*, I wish to ensure that Prince Alberto places his troops at the disposal of my . . . friends. You wish only for the return of the Earl, which is very proper sentiment for a lady." He spread his hands deprecatingly. "You see how closely our interests coincide. You will not wish to throw away the life of your husband for a mere political scruple that affects only the periphery of British interests."

Marianne pressed her hands to her sides in a physical effort to still the whirling mass of thoughts that clogged her brain, stifling rationality and logical conjecture. A lesser intelligence than her own could by now have deduced that the Earl and his uncle were engaged in some clandestine activity on behalf of the Government. The nature of the activity was immaterial. What mattered to Marianne was that she should be taken to the Earl's side so that she could discover for herself the extent of his injuries. The hazards of committing her safety to the uncertain mercies of the *Baron* de Bellevigne were, for the time being, submerged by the need to reassure herself of the Earl's safety.

In an obscure corner of her mind she acknowledged that her obsession with rescuing her husband sprang partly from regret, and partly from a sense of guilt. Whatever the faults of the Earl's character and upbringing, her own behaviour at their first meeting and her coldness since their marriage, had helped to keep them apart. If they had enjoyed a better, more natural relationship—if her own pride had not been so great—more information might have been exchanged between them and the *Baron's* veiled threats would have seemed easier to deal with. As it was, she found herself in a situation in which her ignorance weighted the odds against her, and thus against the Earl's safety.

She turned her back on the *Baron*, so that he could not scrutinize her expression, and spoke haltingly. "You are quite right. I cannot allow considerations of Government policy to interfere with my wifely duties in regard to the Earl." She turned round and looked at the *Baron* with a measure of calculation, uncertain of whether he could be expected to accept the web of lies she planned to spin for his benefit. "Sir Henry Lane is a cautious and experienced member of the Government, well used to conducting . . . delicate . . . negotiations," she said and waited to see if the *Baron* would make any sign that the introduction of this name was a surprise to him. But he remained immobile, his face impassive, with no visible indication of the tension that he must surely be feeling.

Reluctantly, Marianne continued with her improvization. "It is true that the Crown was given to the Earl. It was all arranged on the very day that we were married. You probably know that Sir Henry came round to Rodbourne House after dinner." She paused again, before adding, "I'm sure you will realize that Sir Henry would not entrust such a priceless object to *anyone*—not even his nephew—without taking adequate measures to ensure its safety. Whatever the Earl may have told you, the truth is that *I* possess the only key which will unlock the door to the place where the Crown is hidden, but only the Earl knows where the hiding place is located. Sir Henry deliberately divided the responsibility between us in this fashion so that both of us would have to be present when the King's Cavalry officers came to pick up the Crown for delivery to . . . to Prince Alberto."

The *Baron* de Bellevigne remained silent for a few moments, pulling the Earl's letter meditatively through his fingers. "It is not likely that Sir Henry Lane would draw a woman into his schemes," he said finally.

Marianne shrugged. "That may be true. Sir Henry would not normally have asked the Earl to assist him on the very day that we were married. However, in this case I believe he was desperate for help from some person whom he could trust absolutely." She hoped that this flight of imagination, based on no more than a few minutes spent in conversation with Sir Henry, would not seem unreasonable. Apparently her improvization succeeded, for the *Baron* looked suddenly alert.

"Ah! Then it is as I feared. Claudio's activities are suspected."

He immediately regretted this involuntary confidence, however, for he turned to Marianne and demanded with a brusqueness quite absent from his earlier conversation, "Then you will give me the key, and after I have retrieved the Crown and taken it to a place of safety, the Earl will be returned to you."

"No," said Marianne baldly.

The *Baron* was taken aback. "What do you mean, 'no'?"

Marianne pretended a nonchalance she did not feel. "I am not totally without experience of the world, *Monsieur le Baron*. You are suggesting that I surrender all my knowledge to you and in exchange I receive only a promise, backed by no guarantees. You are not perhaps aware that I come from a long line of successful tradesmen?" She smiled gently. "I'm afraid my commercial training is too deeply ingrained to allow me to make such an unequal bargain. I prefer that you take me to join the Earl, and then I will tell you where you may find the key to the room in which the Crown is hidden."

The *Baron* gave a short burst of incredulous laughter. "You imagine that I would accept such a proposition, *madame*? Once you are reunited with your husband, what possible reason would you have for revealing information that you have gone to such lengths to conceal?"

"Well," said Marianne thoughtfully, "I believe there are several reasons why you must accept my offer. In the first place, I shall be coming with you and I shall thus be putting myself quite in your power. In the second place, you cannot expect to search a family residence, even one the size of Tarrisbroke Hall, without encountering several of the innumerable servants and members of the Earl's family." She smiled without much humour. "Surely even you must cavil slightly at the thought of capturing vast numbers of servants and English aristocrats. If you are hoping to preserve even the smallest element of secrecy about your plans, you can hardly go about burglarizing and terrorizing an entire country estate."

The *Baron* hesitated. "Your absence will be noted, and coupled with the Earl's disappearance, will give rise to precisely the hue and cry that you are urging me to avoid."

"The Earl's absence has already caused considerable speculation, how could it not? But I shall send one of the maids to Smith with a note containing an explanation for

my absence. I shall do it now, so that you may reassure
yourself that I have conveyed no secret instructions." She
moved across to call one of the servants from the kitchen,
but was stopped by the biting pressure of the *Baron's* hands
about her wrists.

"I should mention to you, *Madame*, that I did not leave
myself totally unprotected. My associates have instructions
to . . . dispose of . . . the Earl if I have not returned within
a specified number of hours." His eyes raked Marianne's
white face. "You understand at last, my lady, that I do not
play games where the future of my country is at stake."

"I understand only that I wish to see my husband,
Monsieur. Now would you please release my hands from
your grasp?"

Warily, the *Baron* de Bellevigne did as she requested,
stepping back to observe her movements with watchful
eyes. Marianne opened the small door that led into one of
the sculleries, waiting for the realization of her presence to
spread among the scurrying kitchen maids. Even at this
moment of crisis she could not help noticing how shabbily
and inadequately dressed the young girls were, their hands
swollen with chilblains and their skin grey with the pallor
of insufficient food. She added one more notch to the tally
of complaints against the Dowager Countess, and ran her
eyes over the unprepossessing group of servants who now
waited, in cowed silence, for her to speak. She chose a
dark-haired little girl, probably not more than ten years
old, whose sparkling eyes and clear skin suggested that her
years of drudgery had only just begun.

Marianne smiled at the girl in a friendly fashion. "I have
a message for you to take to Smith, the Earl's valet. Do

you think you can do that?"

The girl looked up doubtfully, swallowing nervously before plucking up courage to speak. "We bain't allowed upstairs, ma'am, your ladyship."

"Well, just this once, I shall give you permission," said Marianne. "I will write it on the note you are to give Smith, and then he will understand that you are doing just as you were asked."

"Yes ma'am, your ladyship."

"What is your name?" asked Marianne.

"Annie, your ladyship," replied the girl, and then hastily, for fear of seeming discourteous, added, "Annie Jones, ma'am, your ladyship."

Marianne beckoned to her to follow, and the other girls watched with awe as Annie walked behind the Countess back into the small room. The *Baron* de Bellevigne waited, as silent and as alert as ever.

Marianne gestured to the housekeeper's old desk. "I cannot write without adequate materials."

The *Baron* ignored the note of defiance in her voice and replied smoothly, "Indeed, I would not expect it. There is a quill and some paper which, though not of the quality normally used by the Countess of Tarrisbroke, will no doubt serve our purpose. There is also some ink that I have taken the liberty of moistening in order to make it serviceable. The excellent Smith will have no difficulty in reading your message."

It was impossible to think of subtle double meanings, with the *Baron* hovering at her elbow. Impossible even to guess what hints Smith might be expected to understand. In despair, Marianne seized her pen and scratched out a message. "The Earl has met with a slight accident, and I am accompanying the Baron de Bellevigne in order to bring him home. Please inform the Dowager Countess, and Miss Thatcher of my whereabouts. Annie has my permission to leave the kitchens in order to deliver to you this note."

She ceased writing and handed the message in silence to the *Baron*. "Who is Miss Thatcher?" he asked.

"My companion."

He read the note several times, and being unable to detect any possible meaning other than the one apparent on the surface, he handed it back to Marianne with a slight, satisfied smile.

"It seems that you are, perhaps, planning to be sensible. But you should add your signature, my lady."

She took the brief note and penned her name, "Marianne, Countess of Tarrisbroke." She stared at the signature, unable to repress a flash of awe that this title was hers, together with the responsibilities that devolved upon the bearer of such an ancient name. She looked at Annie, who stood, thin and awkward, gaping at the two resplendent figures that talked across her head.

"You may take this to Smith's room now, Annie. He will be anxious to know where I am going." She would have said something further, tried—however hopelessly—to convey some verbal message by means of the serving-girl, but the *Baron* raised his hand imperiously, commanding her to silence. Sighing, she handed the message to Annie, pointing to the lines that gave her permission to go upstairs. "If you meet anybody, Annie, you may show them these words here, and they will know that you have permission to run this errand for me."

Annie wiped her greasy hands on the already grease-covered surface of a sackcloth apron, taking the letter by its extreme corner so as to avoid contact with the Countess's soft, white fingers. Seeing the kind smile bestowed upon her by this Celestial Being, she gulped several times for air, then said, "I knows me letters, your ladyship. We'm done learned them at Sunnay School." With a gasp of pride she concluded. "I can write me name—full out."

The *Baron* clicked his tongue in impatience and Marianne smiled. "I'm glad, Annie. Perhaps when the Earl and I return from our travels, we can start a Sunday School here. It would be pleasant if all the boys and girls who work in Tarrisbroke could read, don't you think?"

Annie remained silent, unable to speak in the face of such benevolent promises. She grasped the note for Mr. Smith to her concave bosom and blushed to the roots of her hair. "Thank you, ma'am. Your ladyship. I'll give this 'un to Mr. Smith right away, ma'am. Yes, your ladyship."

The *Baron* de Bellevigne watched her departure with impatience. "It will always remain a mystery to me—this determination of the British labourer to bestow a dog-like devotion upon his master. We have just seen a young girl—impossibly clothed, probably not too well fed—and yet you have only to smile at her and she is your devoted servant for life. While in France the peasants turned upon us and very nearly tore us apart."

Marianne shrugged. "I perceive many possible explanations, *Monsieur*. But I would prefer to discuss them at some other occasion. May I now be taken to join my husband?"

"But of course, *madame*." The *Baron* gripped her hands in his hard clasp. "If you will accompany me to the garden, we may begin our journey."

"But my cloak. . . ."

"Enough, madame. We have wasted time enough and the hour presses. Can you not endure a little chill when so much lies at stake?"

"But how am I to ride in such clothes?" cried Marianne.

The *Baron* pushed her roughly in the small of her back, all pretence at courtesy vanishing under a wave of rage. "You may leave the problems of transportation to me, my lady. But for now, if you wish to see your husband alive, it would be better if you simply started to walk with me. I do not wish to encounter the so-fierce Mr. Smith before some of my ... colleagues ... are a little closer."

The pressure of his hands about her arms increased, and Marianne found herself bundled out into the small passageway that ran the length of the kitchen quarters. With the confidence of a man who knows precisely where he is going, the Baron pulled her stumbling steps briskly along the twists of the corridor until they finally emerged through a small door into a neglected tangle of shrubbery alongside the kitchen garden.

"Our horses are waiting, Lady Tarrisbroke," murmured the *Baron*, and before Marianne had a chance to grasp his purpose, a soft silk handkerchief was drawn across her eyes, binding her into total and impenetrable darkness.

CHAPTER TWELVE

The endless, swaying blackness of the journey ended with a suddenness that threw Marianne against the rough wooden panels of the carriage door. She had long since given up any attempts to remove the blindfold from her eyes, for every time she started to raise her arm the *Baron*'s soft, cool hands grasped her wrists and returned them to her lap. But the sudden jolt startled her so much that her hands flew involuntarily to the silk bandage, only to be seized once again by the *Baron*. "Desist, my lady," he said. "I do not wish to submit you to the ignominy of bound hands."

Marianne ignored his threat. "Are we arrived?" she asked. "Have you brought me to my husband?"

She could hear the impatience in his voice more clearly, now that her eyes were covered. "As I promised, *madame*. Your husband is inside."

She would have replied, begged to be taken to the Earl, but the sound of the carriage door swinging open forestalled her, and a rush of cold night air blew in to fill the interior of the coach. She shivered, partly from cold and partly from fear, while the *Baron* murmured incomprehensible instructions to his servants. She strained to understand his commands, but he chose to use a dialect, some *patois* that seemed barely connected with its parent French.

TARRISBROKE HALL

The talking ceased and Marianne half-rose from her seat, determined to remain a passive victim no longer. One of the *Baron's* hands was immediately placed with mocking gentleness beneath her elbow, the other stretched across her body to enclose both her wrists in the firm circle of his fingers. A fresh tremor, not caused by the cold, ran through Marianne's body as she felt the ruthless exercise of strength that emanated from the slim, elegant fingers. "We may descend from the carriage, if you are cold, my lady." The *Baron* made no effort to conceal his irony now. "One of my . . . servants . . . waits to assist you at the steps."

A flicker of pride came to Marianne's rescue, saving her from further trembling as she passed from the interior of the coach on to the uneven cobblestones of an old courtyard. The *Baron* waited until all sounds from the horses and carriage had faded into the distance, before he motioned to some invisible servant and Marianne felt the blindfold removed from her eyes.

She had expected some scene of desolation, had even visualized some isolated brigands' lair, filled with dangerous outlaws. Instead, she saw the bare yard and whitewashed stones of a typical labourer's cottage, deserted save for one elderly woman who bobbed and smiled and gestured with the exaggerated movements of the congenitally deaf. A frisson of irrational terror shook Marianne, for the silence of the country landscape seemed more hostile than even the most noisome of villains' dens.

The *Baron* smiled, as if satisfied with Marianne's reaction, although she had said nothing at all, and with a sharp tug at her arm he ordered her brusquely to enter the cottage. She walked quickly across the cobblestones, only too happy to obey the *Baron's* comand. Not only did she hope to discover the Earl safely inside the cottage, but she was anxious to be away from the deserted yard, and the black night that was unrelieved by any comfortable huddle of nearby buildings.

The door to the cottage was open and gave immediate access to the living area, a gloomy room with rough stone walls and bare wooden floor, made slightly more comfortable by a small fire burning in the iron grate, and an oil lamp, perched high on the wall, that emitted a smoky and somewhat flickering glow of light. The *Baron* bowed to Marianne. "Well, my lady, you see that I have fulfilled my promise and brought you to your husband."

A dark mass hunched on a sagging couch in the corner of the room stirred into life. With a groan the Earl of Tarrisbroke rolled off the makeshift bed and swung round to face the *Baron*. At the sight of his wife his grey cheeks paled still further. He staggered slightly and would have fallen, if a buxom woman in dirty brown homespun had not grabbed his arm.

Overwhelmed by this evidence of weakness, her eyes transfixed by the red-stained rags that bound up her husband's left arm, Marianne rushed to the Earl's side. For the moment she forgot the presence of the *Baron* and all the dangers he implied, just as she forgot the uneasy ambivalence of the relationship that existed between the Earl and herself. "My lord!" Anxiously she ran her fingers over his pale forehead, feeling the fever that burned beneath the surface of his skin. She drew his right hand to her cheek, pressing her lips against his palm. "Quentin," she said hesitantly, "you must lie down. I am come to look after you." She rested her head briefly against the torn white linen of his shirt, and he crushed her against his body, holding her fiercely with his uninjured right arm. "I feared . . . feared that you were dead," she whispered at last.

"No. Not that." He summoned up the ghost of a laugh. "I have already told my uncle that I am not so easily disposed of! All the same, I wish you had not come."

Marianne smoothed the lumpy cushion that served as his only pillow and attempted to organize the solitary blanket so that it might afford maximum warmth. It was impossible to ignore the dirty rags on the Earl's left arm, and the spreading stain that indicated that his wound still bled freely. "How can you say such things?" she asked with an attempt at lightness. "After only four days of marriage I did not think to be publicly repudiated." She saw his faint smile and added, "Besides, you know, I have come at your own request. You did, after all, write a note begging me to accompany the *Baron* de Bellevigne."

The Earl raised himself on to his right elbow and stared coldly at the *Baron*, who continued to regard Marianne's ministrations in cynical silence. Finally he raised his shoulders in a delicate shrug, acknowledging the unspoken question in the Earl's eyes.

"Yes, my lord Earl. The Countess was shown a note. I was intrigued to find that milady is unfamiliar with her own husband's handwriting. Sad that you have never needed to send her a *billet doux*, is it not? So unlike the way we conduct a romance in France."

"The note was a forgery, of course," said Marianne flatly. "Oh Quentin, I am sorry."

He dismissed her apology with an impatient brush of his

hand. "It is of no consequence. One way or another there is no doubt that the *Baron* would have brought you here. Well, Bellevigne, you appear to have us both in your power. Are we to be told of your plans?"

The *Baron* looked at them both thoughtfully for several silent minutes. The slatternly serving woman poured herself a mug of foaming ale, smacking her lips in evident enjoyment of the drink and with a complete disregard for the tension that stretched with tangible force among the other three people in the room. Finally the *Baron* spoke.

"My plans are very simple, my lord. I wish to find out where the Crown of the Martyr Saint Helen-Theodora has been concealed, and then I wish to remove it to a place of . . . safety. When this purpose has been achieved, you and your wife will be free to go."

"But the Earl needs the services of a surgeon," said Marianne. "Surely we can be permitted to seek help before it is too late?"

The *Baron* ignored her outburst and spoke once again to the Earl. "The Countess was highly distressed when she learned of the sorry state of your health, my lord. You may be interested to know that she has revealed to me the precautions taken by Sir Henry Lane to ensure the safe delivery of this Crown." Marianne could feel the involuntary stiffening of the Earl's body at these words, but he made no comment and the *Baron* spoke with greater impatience. "Come, come, my lord. I know that the Countess possesses the key to the room where the Crown has been hidden, and I am aware of the fact that only you know the location of this room. I wish to have from you complete and detailed instructions for finding this room, and then I shall take your Countess back to Tarrisbroke so that she and I may enter the room together. If you are left here, I retain a perfect guarantee of the Countess's good behaviour."

The Earl laughed weakly. "I did not know that my wife was gifted with such admirable powers of invention—and all worked out on the spur of the moment, too! Alas, *Monsieur le Baron*, I fear that you have been misinformed. The Crown is on its way to Prince Alberto, heavily guarded by a troop of the King's Household Cavalry. My wife—at least I imagine this to be her motive—wished merely to be reunited with me and spun you a tale that she hoped would achieve her objective."

The *Baron* was silent, and paced nervously around the tiny room, showing perturbation for the first time since Marianne had encountered him. Finally he stopped by the couch and peered down at the Earl. "I find your story ridiculous in view of information that I have received from other sources. But I will allow you a short while to ponder what fate I may have in store for you both if I receive no assistance in my search for the Crown." His mouth twisted into a smile. "I am in any case riding out to meet a visitor from London, who is an old acquaintance of yours, my lord. I have no doubt that—between us—we shall be able to devise several methods of persuading you to tell the truth."

"I am sure your methods are very convincing, *Monsieur le Baron*. A French aristocrat who has survived all the changes of regime in France must indeed be possessed of remarkable . . . talents."

For a moment the *Baron*'s temper hovered in the balance, and then he shrugged. "Not the least of those talents, my lord, is an ability to retain control in the face of provocation. You will not find it easy to provoke me into misjudgment."

"Then," said the Earl quietly, "make sure that you do not fall into the trap of not believing *my* words simply because you would prefer them to be untrue."

The *Baron* turned round in the doorway and glanced indifferently at the Earl. "I hope that the Crown is in your possession, my lord, simply because in that way it will be quicker to retrieve it. However, if it should happen to be true that the Crown is already across the Channel, then I hold in my hands two remarkably valuable bargaining counters. I think Sir Henry Lane would be quick to point out to your Government that the price of a few State jewels could not possibly compare with the value of the life of such a prominent member of the British aristocracy. And his wife, of course. So you see—as I told you before—the sooner this treasure is in my hands, the sooner you and your lovely Countess may look forward to returning to the delights of an interrupted honeymoon."

CHAPTER THIRTEEN

The *Baron* closed the main door of the cottage quietly behind him, but the sounds of a heavy key turning in the old iron lock carried quite plainly in the stillness of the night, and Marianne listened in a hypnotized silence to the retreat of his footsteps across the cobblestones.

She ran to the door, twisting the knob uselessly between her fingers and only stopped her futile clawing at the latch when she felt the dirty fingers of the serving woman placed firmly on her arm. The woman gave a shrill whistle, and immediately a burly groom came out of some small room —probably the kitchen—that Marianne saw opened off the side of the living room.

"What's going on?" he enquired brusquely, his voice thick with the local Kentish accent. He looked at Marianne and grinned slyly. "Bain't a bit of use to be carrying on and such like. We'm got the house shut up real cozy like. It do keep out highwaymen and other suchlike villains, don't it Lizzie?" He chuckled heartily, pleased with his own simple joke, and Lizzie looked at him sourly. "You keep your wits about you Ben Dorkins. I want my money, even if you don't." She turned to Marianne and bundled her back to the hearth in the living room. "You'd best settle down, my lady. There bain't any ways for a body to run out of this place."

Marianne walked listlessly across to the Earl. "It was foolish of me to behave in that way." She hesitated for a few seconds, and then added frankly. "I was frightened, but I realize that we cannot possibly escape by using brute force. What plans do you have for us? Is there some way I can help?"

The Earl smiled at her, the warmth in his eyes causing her heart to lurch more violently than any of the Baron's threats, and he gestured almost imperceptibly in the direction of the serving woman. "I think I am too weak to plan daring escapes . . . or even any escape at all. . . ." He leant back against the lumpy pillow and his cheeks seemed so pale that Marianne had a hard time convincing herself that this latest seizure of pain was not genuine.

"I must bandage your wound," she said anxiously and looked defiantly at the servant. "He cannot stay covered in such filthy rags. Will you fetch me some water?" She spoke with the habit of command, so that the woman sat irresolute for only a few seconds before heaving herself out of the comfortable armchair and lumbering over to the kitchen door. "Bain't no use to be trying summat tricky, my lady, because Ben is a-waiting in the kitchen just to hear my call."

Marianne ignored the threat and turned her back on the retreating servant, lifting up the skirts of her overdress and tearing impatiently at the delicate cambric of her petticoat. The Earl watched in silent amusement, and then remarked softly. "It's almost worth being injured, if I am to receive such affectionate ministrations. It is certainly more than I managed to achieve whilst I remained well."

Marianne blushed. "Hush," she said. "There is no time for you to perfect your skill in flirtation, even if it is a new experience to try your charms upon a tradesman's daughter." She tried to look severe. "We have too much to discuss, and too little time. Give me your arm."

Meekly, the Earl extended his injured arm and Marianne unfolded the blood-stained rags. She tried not to shudder at the sight of the mangled flesh that was eventually revealed, but her stomach churned over and she was forced to sit down rather abruptly on the Earl's bed.

He laid his hand over her quivering fingers and said quietly. "There is no need to force yourself into performing tasks that are distasteful to you. I can assure you that my wound is less fearsome than it looks."

Marianne shook her head impatiently. "It is nothing. Of course I must replace this rag with some cleaner dressing." She tried to smile. "It is merely that I am not much in the way of binding up sword slashes." She saw his eyes fixed upon her and said, "How did you come to receive such a wound?"

The Earl fell back once more against the pillows, watching Lizzie as she returned to the room bearing a small pewter bowl of water. Marianne thanked her briefly and immediately began to bathe the jagged edges of the cut, willing herself to ignore the beads of sweat that stood out on the Earl's forehead each time she touched the centre of the wound. The ordeal was over more swiftly than she had feared, and as she bound the strips of cambric over the Earl's arm she asked once more, "How did it happen?"

The Earl replied through clenched teeth, relaxing slightly as the bandaging neared completion and helped deaden the pain in his arm. "It was, I think, quite accidental. I moved suddenly, and the dagger held by my captor grazed my sleeve. As I turned to push him away, the point of the dagger slashed right through my coat. But although the bleeding seems profuse, it is nought but a surface wound and should heal rapidly now I have submitted to your vigorous cleansing treatment."

Their conversation seemed to be of no interest to the servant. Once she saw that her pair of captives made no effort to storm the locked door of the cottage, she paid them little further attention, preferring to sit almost on top of the small fire, nursing her jug of ale and stirring her heavy body only to throw an occasional log on to the fire. Marianne suspected that the woman's brain, fuddled by alcohol and accustomed to hearing Kentish dialect, had difficulty in interpreting a conversation conducted in swift, normal English. In a low voice she asked the Earl, "How did you come to be captured? It must have been inside the house?"

"I entered my room and saw at once that the jewel case had been disturbed. I was not too much troubled, since the whole object of this elaborate plot was to arouse interest in my movements, and in my supposed possession of the Crown. I was relieved that action had occurred so soon, and was only anxious to call Smith and set a search in motion for any strangers who might have been observed in the neighbourhood. The Tarrisbroke estates may be falling into rack and ruin, but my people are still loyal and I did not despair of hearing a description that would have enabled me to identify the intruders.

"But there was no immediate response from Smith and I

stepped out into the corridor, impatient for his arrival and for his help. I was seized from behind, with no chance to see the face of my assailant. He held a dagger to my throat, which I failed to heed as a warning. Hence the wound in my arm." He grimaced in self-mockery. "I was, I'm afraid, bundled ignominiously downstairs and into a carriage that waited in a dark corner of the kitchen gardens."

Marianne interrupted him eagerly. "I, too, was led out through a passageway near the kitchen. It seems an extraordinary place to find a path wide enough to allow passage for a travelling carriage."

The Earl looked acutely embarrassed. "I think the existence of that path is well known to the local populace. My father was in the habit of bringing his . . . female companions right into Tarrisbroke Hall. He felt that by using a service entrance such actions were rendered more acceptable."

Marianne deliberately ignored the Earl's tension. "In that case," she said lightly, "I must remember to order bushes planted along the entire length of the road *immediately* upon our return to Tarrisbroke. Right in the centre of the path." She touched his hand. "And if all else fails, I shall stand sentinel at the kitchen door until I am quite sure that you are safely in your bedchamber . . . alone."

"Not alone, I hope," said the Earl. "But certainly without companions introduced via the kitchen garden."

Marianne felt his eyes searching her face for a few minutes before she turned away. "You have not told me the rest of your story," she said at last.

The Earl sighed. "If you are determined to hear the rest of my sorry tale, I shall be forced to confess that I lost consciousness soon after we entered the carriage and I have no idea in which direction we travelled. I felt a suspicion of salt in the air when they brought me in to this cottage, and it seems reasonable to suppose that the *Baron* would choose a hiding-place that is near to the coast. He must be planning to leave the country almost immediately, since he has not hesitated to reveal his identity. But precisely which of the ports he has selected, I cannot guess. Are you able to enlighten me?"

Marianne shook her head regretfully. "I was blindfolded during the journey, and anyway I do not know this part of the country. Even if we had travelled in plain daylight, I doubt if I should be able to find my way back to Tarrisbroke. We are a sorry couple, are we not?"

"Not very able conspirators, certainly." The Earl appeared lost in thought. "If only we knew who was behind these plots, it might be easier to make some plans for escape."

Marianne hastened to describe her encounter with the young man in the Earl's bedchamber. "His appearance was not distinctive," she said finally as she floundered over a description of the intruder. "But from his manner of speaking, I did wonder if he came from the Italian peninsula."

The Earl sat up straight on his couch, giving a small exclamation of astonishment before catching the suspicious gaze of the serving woman and sinking back into his former listless posture.

"I believe you have described Claudio di Mazaretto, the brother of Maria Gabrie . . . the brother of a former acquaintance of mine. I did not know Mazaretto had been appointed to Sir Henry's staff, or I should have warned my uncle to exercise the utmost caution. Di Mazaretto has been an ardent admirer of Napoleon Bonaparte from the beginning, and I knew that he wanted to prevent his cousin Prince Alberto from continuing his support of the British. King Louis' position is perilously shaky, and Prince Alberto's defection at this precise moment would be one more pillar removed from the monarchy's system of supports."

"I'm glad that my story seems significant to you," said Marianne. "But even if the young man *was* di Mazaretto, I do not see that it helps us to escape from here."

The Earl appeared to give no heed to her rather fractious remark, raising his hand to his head and emitting a deep groan. Terrified, Marianne leaned over to place her hand on his brow, only to find herself clutched with some firmness in a position that entirely screened the Earl's head and shoulders from the servant's view. He whispered quickly. "I have some sort of a plan. Bring the servant over here, and get her to bring the jug of ale."

Marianne turned flustered eyes in the direction of the serving woman. "Lizzie!" she called distractedly. "Lizzie! The Earl has taken a turn for the worse, what are we to do?" She watched impatiently as the nurse dragged her reluctant body out of the chair, wringing her hands in a credible imitation of a nervous female at the end of her tether. "Bring the ale! Bring the ale! We must try and get him to drink. I believe he is quite unconscious."

Lizzie looked very doubtful at the prospect of wasting good ale on a man too far gone to know what he was drinking, but in the end she decided to obey Marianne's commands, the journey to the kitchen for fresh drinking water being more arduous than the sacrifice of a little—a very little—of her good beer. She lumbered up to peer at the Earl out of short-sighted eyes, inspecting the shallow rise and fall of his chest with ghoulish satisfaction. "He bain't too hearty, my lady. That I will say." She leant over to feel his forehead, and Marianne seized the jug of ale. "Here! Let me pour him a drink," she said quickly. "You must raise his head up. I am not strong enough."

The servant parted with the precious jug, grumbling quietly as she did so. Marianne waited until the woman turned her back in order to heave the Earl's weight up on to her arm then, neatly and precisely, she hit the servant firmly on the top of her skull. Lizzie found time to emit a small grunt of astonishment, before sliding down into an untidy heap across the bed.

Marianne examined her handiwork with some pride, not attempting to move the servant's body until the Earl ventured a strangled gasp. "I shall faint in reality if you do not move this weight from my lungs soon!"

Full of apologies, Marianne tugged obligingly at the servant's body. Two hundred pounds of solid flesh sagged a little deeper on to the couch. In despair, Marianne turned to the Earl, ignoring the laughter that crinkled the corners of his eyes. "It is all very well for you to laugh. I cannot see how we are to proceed with your brilliant plans for an escape with this . . . this . . . elephant strewn across your lap."

"Pull up that wooden chair," said the Earl obligingly, "and if you place it at the foot of the bed, we can topple her into it. With any luck the *Baron* will not even notice that she is unconscious. She hardly moves even when she is awake."

Marianne, with some assistance from the Earl, propped

TARRISBROKE HALL

Lizzie up in the wooden chair and replaced the jug—its contents sadly depleted—in the cradle of her lap. "There!" said Marianne. "Perhaps when she regains consciousness she will not even realize what we did."

The Earl smiled. "It is very pleasant to plot one's escape with such an optimistic companion. Personally, I hope we are gone long before she returns to the land of the living. Now that we may talk freely, let us make haste and decide what we should do. The Crown is already in Europe. I was not lying when I spoke thus to the *Baron*, although in retrospect I feel it might have been more sensible to conceal this fact from him."

Marianne spoke worriedly. "If we do not have the Crown, we are without bargaining tools. And I don't trust the *Baron* to house us indefinitely if we are serving no useful purpose. It would be all too easy to arrange a convenient carriage accident that would dispose of us both and leave the *Baron* free to pursue the more pressing aspects of his plan."

"Preventing the British Government from passing the Crown to Prince Alberto can only be a small part of his schemes," agreed the Earl. If Bellevigne is interested in Prince Alberto's actions, it can only be because the Bonapartists plan an early uprising against King Louis. Perhaps, impossible as it seems, they even plan for Bonaparte's return from Elba."

Marianne twisted her hands nervously. "It seems to become more and more important for us to escape, and my mind becomes increasingly blank the more I try to delve into it." Her nervousness was increased by a sudden low grunt emanating from the direction of the serving woman, but the Earl reassured her.

"Don't worry, Marianne. She is still unconscious." He swung his legs off the bed and walked with remarkable steadiness over to the casement window. "I think we must not allow ourselves to exaggerate the importance of the Baron's scheming," he said as he peered out into the unrelieved blackness of the night. "I don't think that the fate of Europe hangs in the balance merely because we cannot immediately think of any way to escape. I should dearly love to turn the tables upon Bellevigne, however, if we could devise some method for catching him off-guard." He frowned and fell silent for a few seconds. "I think we have to accept that we cannot escape from here by force. So, if we wish to leave, we shall have to persuade the *Baron* to take us with him."

"We must convince him that the Crown is in Tarrisbroke Hall," said Marianne. "We must pretend that you lied and that it is not already safely on its way to Prince Alberto."

"Bellevigne would never be unwise enough to take us right into Tarrisbroke. God knows, he is no fool and he realizes as well as we do that it would be quite impossible for three or four people to clamber around the Hall without alerting at least a dozen servants to our presence. Particularly since my family and staff must now be worried by our mysterious disappearance. No, that will not do." He stifled a sudden exclamation of mild triumph. "I have it! There is an old family chapel west of the Home Farm woods. That is just the sort of place in which one might decide to hide a priceless relic, and from our point of view it has the advantage of being fairly close to the Hall."

The Earl stepped back from the window and disposed

himself quickly upon the couch. "It is too late for more elaborate plans," he said. "A travelling chaise is even now drawing into the yard. Encourage the *Baron* to believe that my condition has worsened, but remember that in fact I feel stronger by the moment."

"I hope we may find some more potent advantage on our side than such a fragile deception," said Marianne, and collapsed in a convincing heap of weeping womanhood across the Earl's hard couch, just as the sound of approaching footsteps heralded the return of Bellevigne and his companion.

CHAPTER FOURTEEN

A gust of wind blew straight on to Lizzie's face, and the noise as the *Baron* slammed the door shut behind him caused her to stir uneasily, her head lolling from one side to the other as she struggled back in semi-consciousness. Bellevigne looked at her in disgust, then spoke sharply to his companion.

"It is a blessing, Claudio, that I do not rely upon you for the selection of too many of our hirelings, or we should find ourselves ill-served. It is fortunate that Ben Dorkins and the other old crone can be relied upon to remain sober."

The young man shrugged his shoulders. "Drunk or sober, it makes no odds. I do not see where you expect Tarrisbroke to go, wounded and without horses." He walked over to Marianne pulling her up none too gently from the Earl's side. He executed a low bow, his eyes sliding over her dishevelled appearance with mocking insolence.

"It is indeed a pleasure to see you again, my lady. Such devotion is touching to observe. However, the object of your attentions scarcely deserves so great a loyalty." He glared at the Earl. "I wish my dagger had done more than wound you, my lord. I have longed these many months to have the opportunity of running my sword through your treacherous body."

The Earl spoke with lazy indifference. "I am amazed, my dear Mazaretto, to have aroused such ire, even in one known for his—er—volatile humour. May I be allowed to enquire what I have done to incur such wrath?"

"You mock me," said Claudio di Mazaretto. "Do you hope to deny that you dishonoured my sister, the *Principessa* Maria Gabriella? That you made her name a subject of gossip in half the courts of Europe?"

"My dear Mazaretto, I had no idea that my simple pursuits were followed with any interest at all in *any* of the Courts of Europe, but I must certainly bow to your superior knowledge in such matters. However, I assure you that it was not possible for me to *dishonour* the *Principessa*. Our affaire, pleasant as it was, merely represented a brief interlude in Maria Gabriella's perpetual romantic adventures." He looked quite kindly at di Mazaretto and said gently, "I was not your sister's first lover, *Signor Conte*. And I feel quite certain that I shall not be the last."

With a cry of rage the young *Conte* sprang towards the Earl, ready to seize the Earl's throat between his fingers, but he was stopped by a curt command from the *Baron*. "Desist Claudio! Your personal revenge is of no consequence at the moment." He turned to the Earl and examined the white face upon the pillow with complete detachment. "I trust that your wife has persuaded you to be more sensible, my lord? I see that she has rebound your wound, but I cannot say that the general state of your health looks much improved. Would you now care to tell me where I may find the Crown that is causing us all so much unnecessary inconvenience?"

"Damn you to hell!" said the Earl deliberately. "Even if I am dying, you will not persuade me to reveal its hiding place."

"Very noble," said the *Baron* approvingly. "But I am not intending anything as crude as your murder, my lord. Such a very ineffectual means of pursuing my objective, would you not agree?" He examined Marianne with meditative interest. "There are other methods that would be so much more certain of producing the desired results and at infinitely less risk to myself. For example, how would you feel if I escorted your fair Countess into the bedroom and there tied her hands securely behind her, before offering Claudio his revenge? You may not be prepared to bargain for your own life, my lord, but perhaps you may feel a little more strongly about your wife's honour?"

Marianne turned white. "No, you could not." She looked pleadingly at di Mazaretto. "*Signor Conte*, you would not wish to exact such retribution. . . ."

The Earl dragged himself to his feet as the silence lengthened. "There is no need to pursue your threats, Bellevigne." He laughed harshly. "You interpret my character too well. I will tell you where the Crown is hidden, but not until I receive word from my servants that my wife has been returned to Tarrisbroke unharmed."

"Oh no, my lord. You must think me simple indeed. When we return your good lady to her home, we are once again in the position of having no effective guarantee of your good behaviour. The safety of your own person, which I suspect you value little, offers me no security."

"But his safety means everything to me," said Marianne. "I did not marry into the peerage in order to find myself a dowager before my first season in town! I will not permit the Earl to throw his life away to protect a collection of jewels for some foreign nobody." She glanced scornfully at the *Conte* di Mazaretto and noted his flush of anger with great satisfaction. The more enraged their antagonists, the less likely they were to make sensible judgments. "My lord, you *must* listen to me." She turned to the Earl in an attitude of supplication. "Let us go with these men to the Crown's hiding place. I will give them the key if *you* will disclose the location of the Crown to the *Baron*." She allowed her voice to break on a little sob. "Does my happiness mean so little to you? Is some paltry government alliance more important to you than my life . . . my honour?"

The Earl spoke wearily. "It is my duty to protect you, Marianne, and to try to make you happy. But I also have a duty to Sir Henry—and to the King."

The *Conte* spoke contemptuously. "A mad King and a libertine Prince Regent? It is to such people that you owe your loyalties?"

"This conversation is pointless," said the *Baron* impatiently. "I do not intend to allow you from this cottage until I have the Crown in my own hands. Time presses, and I wish you to understand, my lord, that I shall not hesitate to carry out my threats."

The Earl sighed. "It seems to me, *Monsieur le Baron*, that we must each trust the other a little if we are to find some acceptable way out of this impasse. The Crown *is* on my estate—you see that finally I acknowledge the truth—but it is not in the Hall. I shall agree to escort you to its hiding place and I will remain as your hostage while the

Conte di Mazaretto escorts my wife back into Tarrisbroke Hall in order to pick up the key."

"Fine planning, my lord. But I am not so foolish as you seem to think. What is to prevent your wife alerting a dozen strong servants and sending them out to effect your release?"

"The key is not hidden in my room," said Marianne suddenly. Hesitantly she pulled at the fine twists of golden chain suspended around her neck, and from the bodice of her gown she withdrew a small key. "The Crown is in a cupboard that is locked with this key," she said. "We do not need to go inside the Hall. You will be able to take the Crown and will have ridden off with it, long before we are able to alert the servants to our presence."

The Earl looked at Marianne somewhat sadly, as if regretting her betrayal of so many government secrets. "Ah, Marianne! And what is to prevent the *Baron* placing a bullet between our shoulders once he has found the Crown?"

Marianne gave a little cry. "Oh no, my lord! They could not do such a thing." Terrified, she turned imploringly to the Baron. "You will let us go once you have the Crown, you will not . . . hurt us, will you?"

"I give you my word upon it," said the *Baron* smoothly, and Marianne expelled her breath in a trusting sigh.

"And you will forgive me, Quentin, for betraying your uncle's little secrets?" Coquettishly she ran her fingers over his cheek. "We have all our lives together still ahead of us. We cannot count the importance of some old half-forgotten relic, can we?"

The Earl's expression was not easy to interpret. "I would

not expect a woman to understand the significance of this Crown," he said finally. He patted Marianne rather patronisingly on the arm. "I will see that you do not come to any harm, my dear." He paused and the other occupants of the room could see how his body swayed and the vigorous effort he exerted to sit down again upon his couch without falling. Marianne rushed to his side, tenderly stroking his brow and staring reproachfully at the *Baron* and the *Conte* di Mazaretto. "You see," she said accusingly. "He is so weak and you force him to stand and argue the issue with you. What do I care about silly government plans? Make the carriage comfortable for us and we shall be on our way. You shall get your Crown and I shall be at liberty to seek the services of a surgeon for my husband. *That* is all I care for."

The *Baron* looked at her doubtfully, but the *Conte* interrupted impatiently before Bellevigne could speak.

"Come, Bellevigne, we cannot afford to wait any longer. The boat has been ready any time these past two days, and we cannot expect a favourable wind to hold for ever." He saw that the *Baron* still hesitated, and he gave vent to a sharp exclamation. "You waste valuable time, Bellevigne. We have all the journey to make our plans, and to smooth out any rough points in our protection. *Dio mio, che timidita!* What do you expect one injured man and a slip of a woman to accomplish against us? An ambush, perhaps?"

The *Baron* spoke coldly. "If this is how you and your countrymen plan a campaign, it is small wonder that your provinces have for so long been under the domination of foreign rulers. Be silent, so that I may think!"

Marianne, who saw Lizzie stirring once again, got up hastily from her devoted position by the Earl's bedside. "Oh la, sirs! My husband has fainted clear away. What are we to do if he is unconscious when we need directions?"

The *Baron* came to a final decision. "It will be dawn within three hours, so it is true that we cannot delay." Impatiently he dragged a flask of brandy from his hip pocket and forced the mouth of the bottle between the Earl's lips. "Ben," he yelled, in the direction of the kitchen. "Come and take the Earl to his carriage. You, my lady, may come with me. Claudio, attend to the horses and see that Pierre and Matthieu are ready to accompany us." His lips tautened in an unpleasant smile. "There is no need for a blindfold this time, my lady. You will need all your faculties alert if you are to keep your husband alive long enough to be of assistance to us all. And it matters little to me that you will discover how close this hideaway is to the boundaries of Tarrisbroke. I have no further use for the cottage now."

Marianne allowed herself to be bundled roughly from the room, casting one helpless look at her husband, who leaned weakly against Ben Dorkins' stout but unfriendly shoulder. He swayed, as if hovering on the very borderline of consciousness . But when Marianne took an involuntary step backwards in order to help him, the *Baron* grabbed her arm and pushed her out into the courtyard. "Save your tenderness for the journey, my lady. Your husband will have need of it all."

CHAPTER FIFTEEN

Helen Thatcher paced up and down her small, damp room. The temperature of the bedchamber was arctic, but this was not the reason for her restlessness, even though she spared an occasional moment to reflect adversely on the sort of accommodation Lady Eleanor considered suitable for paid companions. For the fifteenth time, she walked over to her window, pulling back the faded draperies to peer out through the unrelieved gloom of the night. When her earnest squinting produced no results, she plumped herself down on to the bed, crinkling the sensible grey stuff of her morning gown between agitated fingers.

The light tap at her door was a welcome relief and she ran to open it. Smith was standing on the threshold, looking as neat and self-possessed as ever, showing no signs of his hurtling ride to London.

"Oh Smith! Have you found Sir Henry? What news?"

"I very much regret, Miss, that I was unable to speak personal with Sir Henry seeing as how Sir Henry is at this moment travelling to Dover, in readiness for his departure tomorrow for foreign parts." He saw Miss Thatcher's crest-fallen expression and added more cheerfully, "I did, however, take the liberty of calling upon Mr. Packenham who, being the Earl's oldest and best friend, might be able to add some light to our enquiries. He is waiting downstairs, and would be happy to talk to you in the Library, if you was wishful of joining him."

"But of course. I shall come immediately. You see that I am already dressed for action. I hope, Smith, that you are not utterly exhausted by such a long ride?"

"Twelve hours in the saddle is not my preferred way of spending time, Miss. But during our years in Europe, the Master and I became accustomed to long hours of riding." Descending from his lofty pinnacle for a moment, he added confidingly, "Shocking roads they have over on the Continent, Miss. You wouldn't hardly credit what passes for a carriage road in Spain and Italy. Nothing but mule tracks, covered with flies—not to mention the bandits and brigands, all so starving they'd cut your throat for a crust of bread."

"Yes," said Miss Thatcher, feeling that talk of bandits and brigands was not the most encouraging topic in the circumstances. "Well, we must be thankful that the toll roads in England are maintained in such good order."

She hurried down the stairs, clutching a candle to light her way down the dark recesses of the curved staircase, and managed to recognize the library by its massive, nail-studded oak doors. She peeped cautiously round one of these and gave a sigh of relief when she observed the comforting and stolid figure of Giles Packenham, standing in a relaxed attitude before the fireplace.

She came into the room and held out her hand in warm greeting. "Oh, Mr. Packenham, you cannot *know* how pleased I am to see you here. I am so glad that Smith was sensible enough to ask you to come, and that you were generous enough to accompany him."

Mr. Packenham, who was never the most articulate of men, seemed somewhat taken aback by the warmth of her welcome. "I am happy to be of service to you, Miss Thatcher," he murmured. "Can you tell me in what way I may assist you? Smith was so urgent in his need to return immediately to Tarrisbroke that he told me little more than that the Earl was missing. I gather that he has not returned during the long hours of our ride?"

"Oh no! Indeed he has not. And with Marianne gone, I have been almost beside myself with worry." She drew a deep breath, forcing herself to be calm. "I am sorry, sir," she said more naturally. "You must be receiving a very false impression of me. I can assure you that in normal circumstances I am far from being an hysterical female. But I have felt so isolated in my fears—so alone—that your welcome presence has caused me to throw normal decorum to the winds."

"Come and sit by the fire, Miss Thatcher," he said soothingly, as he tucked her hand under his arm. "You see, your fingers are like chips of ice. Let me pour you a glass of this excellent sherry, and when you are a little more warmed you may tell me what has occurred. I gather from your state of agitation that the Countess is also missing? We rode so fast that Smith has told me almost nothing."

Miss Thatcher sipped at the sherry and felt a pleasant tingle spread through her body. The worries of the past hours seemed suddenly of much less account, and she was able to explain the mysterious disappearance of the Earl, and then the Countess, in a calm and coherent fashion. "The Dowager Countess and the Lady Eleanor insisted at first that there was no cause for alarm. Even so, I could see that Marianne was troubled by her husband's absence, although she did not discuss it with me. We have known one another so long that we often interpret the other's feelings, even without an opportunity for private discussion." She fumbled in the pocket of her gown and retrieved a crumpled scrap of paper. "When Smith brought me this note, my worst forebodings were realized. Marianne is normally so clear-headed that I cannot allow myself to believe that she would willingly go rushing off across the countryside without making any effort to indicate the direction in which she is going." Worriedly she twisted the sherry glass round in her hands. "And why have they not returned? Even if the Earl cannot be moved, there is no reason why Marianne should not send a messenger, thus setting all our minds at rest. I have never known Marianne to be indifferent to the feelings of others—she is always the most thoughtful of females."

Mr. Packenham patted Miss Thatcher's arm, reassuring her with an easy informality that would have astonished them both had they taken the time to notice it. "You do not have to convince me that all is not well, Miss Thatcher. Quite apart from your own worries, it is clear that Smith entertains similar fears or he would not have bothered to seek me out. It is not easy to shake Smith's imperturbable spirit, so his anxieties are genuine cause for alarm."

Miss Thatcher cleared her throat nervously. "I am *so* relieved to hear you speak in such a fashion, but . . . but . . . I feel it is only honest for me just to mention to you that Marianne was very much opposed to the idea of this marriage. Just at first you know." She looked at Mr. Packenham with some embarrassment. "However, I am quite certain in my own mind that Marianne would never choose to run off in such a hurly-burly fashion, whatever her feelings may have been about the marriage."

Mr. Packenham looked astonished. "My dear Miss Thatcher, there was no possibility in the world that I would have entertained such notions about the Countess of Tarrisbroke. And what have the Countess's feelings about her marriage to do with the *Earl's* disappearance? Are you expecting me to believe that they both decided to slip off and cut their losses?"

"No. Not at all. Oh dear." Miss Thatcher looked increasingly self-conscious. "I thought it better to bring the matter up, because if you should chance to encounter the Dowager, you will find that she believes the Earl's absence is all part of some plot of Marianne's." She saw Mr. Packenham's incredulous expression and said hastily, "Let us talk no more of it. I just wished you to be informed of the Dowager's opinion."

"Yes, indeed," said Mr. Packenham, thankful that he was apparently not expected to comment on this latest aberration of the Dowager. "Er . . . fortunately I believe I must set out from Tarrisbroke before the Dowager is likely to be up," he said in tones of acute relief. "We shall organize search parties that must be ready to set out at first light. And we must send for Smith immediately so that he can tell us everything he knows about the situation."

The Earl's valet, summoned by a sleepy night footman, willingly expounded the theories he had been evolving during the hours of his master's absence.

"I am sure the Earl was doing another job for his uncle, Sir Henry Lane, and the Countess thought that too. She told me so before she disappeared with this *Baron* de Bellevigne fellow."

"Do you know for certain that Sir Henry had asked your master to undertake some task for him?" asked Mr. Packenham.

"Well, sir, one of Sir Henry's secretaries came round to Rodbourne House just before we left for Tarrisbroke. And Sir Henry himself called on his lordship the very day we was married." Smith hunched his shoulders and spoke huffily. "Unfortunately, his lordship didn't choose to confide in me the subject which was discussed with Sir Henry. His lordship has a lamentable bad habit of telling me what he's been up to when it's too late for me to stop him risking his life. I *had* hoped that now we was married we might take our personal safety a bit more into account. We're getting too old for all this racketing about, sir. It's time we settled down and had some children."

"Yes. Quite," said Mr. Packenham, uncertain whether to take the latter part of the speech at its face value or to assume that Smith's identification with his employer was complete. "However, even if we knew exactly what the Earl and Sir Henry were planning to do, I'm not sure that we should achieve very much. Something has clearly gone wrong with everybody's plans." He thought for a few moments in silence. "I can really suggest nothing more constructive than mustering all the men from the estate and organizing search parties in every direction. You have no idea where the *Baron* arrived from, I suppose, Smith?"

"No," said the valet regretfully. "But if this scheme had something to do with the foreigners Sir Henry is always working with, I think they'd be making for the coast if anything went wrong with their plans. Don't you agree, sir?"

"Well, I don't know," said Mr. Packenham cautiously. "It might be worth concentrating greater numbers of men along the paths leading to the coastal roads. I think my own task must be to take the fastest horse in Quentin's stables and ride for Dover. We must bring Sir Henry here, I think, if we are to have any real chance of tracing the Earl's movements."

Miss Thatcher sighed. "And I can see that my lot is the unenviable one of keeping the Dowager Countess and Lady Eleanor tolerably happy. They changed from a mood of sublime optimism at lunch time yesterday to a mood of darkest pessimism by the time dinner was served. They now expect the Earl's body to be returned to them on a slab from moment to moment."

"Do not despair, Miss Thatcher." She felt the warm pressure of Mr. Packenham's fingers clasping her hands. "We shall have found them before the day is out, even if I have to run Quentin's prime cattle into the ground in order to catch up with Sir Henry." He turned to the valet. "I shall leave the organization of the search parties in your capable hands, Smith. I am away to the stable to take my pick." He grinned wryly at Miss Thatcher. "Wish me good fortune, ma'am, for if I should lame one of Quentin's favourite mounts I may decide to set sail for France without ever returning! It would certainly be a safer course than facing Quentin's wrath."

Miss Thatcher was conscious of heightened colour and a heart beating more swiftly than was altogether proper in a maiden lady past the first blush of youth. "Naturally we wish you a safe and swift journey," she said. "I—we—shall look forward to your return."

Mr. Packenham and the valet hurried from the room, leaving Helen Thatcher to stare out of the window at the first faint grey light of dawn. "Marianne," she whispered. "Don't give up. We are going to find you soon."

CHAPTER SIXTEEN

The coachman led the horses into a small thicket of trees and bushes, concealing the carriage from the eyes of any chance passer-by. The Baron, not trusting the obvious air of desolation that surrounded the abandoned chapel, called the remaining groom to his side and issued a few curt instructions. Stolidly the man moved round to the back entrance of the chapel, mounting a watchful and rather ridiculous guard over the deserted footpath that led off in the direction of the Home Farm.

The Earl lay on a blanket under the shelter of the chapel porch, and Marianne knelt down beside him, trying not to focus her eyes on the perpetually spreading red stain that wet the fresh bandage she had applied to his arm only minutes before. The journey from the cottage had taken less than an hour, but it had required all Marianne's courage to retain her optimism in the face of the Earl's increasing weakness. She tried to remember his words of encouragement, to tell herself that she was not familiar with sword-wounds, and that she had no way of judging how much of the Earl's weakness was feigned, how much of it a true reflection of his state of health. However, she knew that the grey pallor of his cheeks was real and that the blood seeping from the jagged cut was weakening him with the passage of every moment. Now that they were actually here, outside the chapel, she wondered what advantage they had possibly hoped to gain by suggesting such a ploy. The Crown was not in the chapel, and no amount of wishful thinking was going to make it appear there.

Claudio di Mazaretto looked indifferently at the wounded man and glanced up to find Marianne's eyes fixed scornfully upon him. He laughed harshly. "You are shocked, my lady, by my indifference to imminent death. But I have seen too many men die far more horribly than your husband. A simple sword wound has lost its terrors for me."

The *Baron* de Bellevigne interrupted before Marianne could reply. "Enough, Claudio." He turned to the Earl. "I wish for instructions, my lord, on the precise location of the Crown."

"No," said the Earl. "I do not trust you to keep your word. For all I know your hired ruffians may have instructions to murder us as soon as the Crown is in your possession. You must leave your pistols out here and *I* will open the room that holds the Crown while my wife holds your daggers."

Claudio di Mazaretto laughed quietly. "So that she may run us through? You jest, my lord Earl."

The *Baron* raised his hand. "There is no danger from the Countess. She could not possibly overpower us both. The Earl shall show us where the Crown is hidden and then he and his Countess can retreat from the Chapel while we retrieve the jewels. Such a scheme offers both parties some measure of security."

The Earl, leaning heavily on Marianne's arm, raised himself from the ground and stood propped up against the chapel wall. "I should like to remind you, gentlemen, that we are now on my estates. And although I have no doubt that your servants could murder us as we emerge from the chapel, the chances of your escaping from my lands without pursuit are slim. It is almost dawn, and I have no doubt that search parties are even now being prepared to scour the grounds."

Marianne stiffened, wondering if the Earl had concocted this elaborate plan with no better hope of rescue than a chance encounter with the members of a search party. His hand tightened on her arm with reassuring pressure, as he turned back to the *Baron*. "I think it is better if you place your pistols on the ground now, and we may then proceed into the chapel. You, *Signor Conte*, had better carry the lamp and find somewhere secure to rest it once we are inside."

The chapel doors were not locked, and Marianne found her feet making a soft shirring sound on the carpet of autumn leaves that had blown on to the stone slab floor through the open doors and the missing panes in the leaded windows. The flickering light of their lamp illuminated the bright colours of the stained glass windows, casting an eerie red glow about the small procession. They had reached less than half-way down the short aisle when the Earl stopped. "You will stay here," he said. "*Monsier le Baron* and *Signor Conte*, I should be grateful if you would hand over to the Countess the daggers that I imagine to be hidden beneath the folds of your coats."

He waited in silence as the *Conte* and the *Baron* each drew out a small sword and handed it to Marianne. The Earl gave a quick laugh. "I do not believe for one moment that you have surrendered all your weapons," he said. "But if you make any effort to attack my wife while I am opening up the hiding place that conceals the Crown, you will never discover what you seek."

The *Baron* spoke softly. "You seem very certain that we could not find this Crown, my lord. The chapel is small and I have three other men ready to assist me."

"That is true." The Earl sounded amused. "However, my uncle and I exercised considerable caution in selecting a hiding place for such a priceless relic. This chapel is old, as you can see. In fact, it dates from the time of the English Reformation when my ancestors were foolhardy enough to remain faithful to the Catholic religion for two or three generations after the rest of the county had decided it was easier to become Protestant as the King commanded. It therefore has a priest's hole, in common with many buildings which date from that era. I think you would have to tear the building down, stone by stone, before you discovered which of these particular granite blocks covers empty space and not solid wall. The Crown is well protected."

Claudio di Mazaretto acknowledged defeat. "We waste precious time, my lord. Your wife holds our swords. We are waiting for you to show us the door to the hiding place."

The Earl came and stood by Marianne, putting his arm round her shoulder in a gesture she found hard to interpret. Was he offering reassurance? Comforting her? Bidding farewell? Her mind refused to grapple with the implications of this last thought, so she merely looked at him with a calmness she did not feel and asked, "What would you wish me to do, my lord?"

Unbelievably he smiled, and reached down to kiss her cheek. "I would wish you to call me Quentin," he said softly. "But for the moment, I would also wish you to stand a little further away from our friends." He smiled urbanely at the *Baron*. "If the Countess stands here and you remain at a distance, you may observe all my actions and I do not have to worry about what will happen to the Countess when I turn my back."

"We are rooted to the spot," said the *Baron* ironically. "Please do not delay further."

Marianne's breath seemed to be coming in small gasps of fright. She hardly felt the weight of the small swords that she carried, although at first they had seemed intolerably heavy. The Earl walked steadily along the remainder of the aisle, crossed the altar rail and went up to the sacristy steps. He turned aside at the altar table, ignoring the dull metal gleam of the Cross that still surmounted the bare stone table. He paused directly in front of the ornately painted and sculpted wall that decorated the rear of the altar.

"If you will look towards your left, my lords, you will see that when I press the harp of this stone angel, a door will open in the wall. The door conceals a small room in which the consecrated vessels and vestments needed by itinerant priests were once stored. You already hold my wife's key to the cupboard inside the room."

Marianne held her breath. Even the short gasps for air now seemed to be too great an effort. The *Baron* and the *Conte* leaned forward, one of them uttering a cry of excitement as a narrow door opened in the wall, swinging out in such a fashion that any contents of the tiny room were concealed from their view.

The Earl spoke quickly. "I do not advise you to run forward, my lords," but his words were ignored as, with eager impatience, the *Baron* and the *Conte* both pushed forward towards their prize.

As they started to run, there was a slight click, a sudden crash, and Marianne watched almost mesmerised, as the *Baron* and his companion disappeared into a gaping black hole that had opened up in the middle of the aisle floor. An ominous thump was followed by a cry of mingled pain and fright, and then there was only silence.

The Earl slumped against the wall, beads of sweat standing out on his forehead. "Be careful how you walk, Marianne. The mechanism which operates the floor-trap is as old as the priest's hole, and probably faulty."

She ran to the trap door, leaving the heavy swords on the wooden pew, and peered into the impenetrable blackness of the pit. "How did you do it, Quentin? Do you think they are . . . they are. . . ." She swallowed hard. "Do you think they are dead?"

"I will go and look more closely in a moment. The pit beneath that slab is over ten feet deep, but when I was a boy it was invariably left partially filled with straw and leaves, just in case of an accident. I could not be certain that the old mechanism would still work, but it was a gamble I had to take. It is easier to decide to be ruthless when no other chance of escape exists."

Marianne walked quickly away from the dark pit. "I hope they will survive. Their death seems a very . . . final . . . solution to our problems." She reached his side and could not resist resting her head against his shoulder.

The Earl ruffled her hair with one hand. "There is no need for me to remind you, I suppose, that they would certainly have killed us without a second thought as soon as the Crown was in their hands?"

Marianne shuddered. "I prefer not to think about it." She turned away self-consciously. "When I lived in India I became an expert in the art of not thinking about the cruelties of life around me. It has become a constant habit, I fear."

The Earl pulled her gently against him. "We are not yet free of danger by any means. The men outside will not remain standing there indefinitely." He held her at arms' length and said, "Marianne, do you think you can travel back to the Hall alone?" He smiled wryly. "I am not sure that I could manage the journey, and somebody must remain here to barricade the chapel against the *Baron*'s servants."

"Quentin! Your wound! It *is* troubling you, as I thought it was. Let me tend to it!"

"No," he said. "There is no time, Marianne. I must let you out of the side door in the vestry before the sun rises any higher. Already there is sufficient light for you to be seen if either of those two servants chances to glance in your direction. Tread as quietly as you possibly can, Marianne. And let us hope that *somebody* in Tarrisbroke has had the sense to organize a search party. I do not like to think of you tramping six miles back to the Hall. You must be almost at the point of exhaustion."

"It is no matter." Impatiently Marianne brushed his words aside. "But what of you? How are you to prevent the *Baron's* servants entering the Chapel?"

"I shall lock the doors, my dear, and offer repeated prayers that wood around the locks and hinges may not be rotten. Fortunately I am in the best possible place for hoping that my prayers will be answered."

Marianne tried to smile. "I shall be as quick and as silent as possible." Shyly she reached up to brush his lips with a swift kiss. "I will be back with a surgeon, my lord. You will be careful?"

The Earl's dark eyes were lit with tender laughter. "In all our long acquaintance, have you ever known me to be otherwise?" He placed his fingers over her lips when she would have protested and led her into the tiny vestry. Marianne pulled back the rusted iron lock on the door, cutting her fingers and tearing her nails as she did so, but she knew that the Earl had no strength to spare for the task. The grey sky was already lighting up with a yellow-white haze towards the east and the Earl leaned forward for a brief minute to say, "Hurry! And keep your back to the sun. You should find a footpath within a hundred yards of the chapel."

Marianne slipped into the darkness of the small woods, thankful that it offered her protection from prying eyes. In the distance she could hear the restless stomping of the carriage horses, growing increasingly faint as she penetrated deeper into the thicket. Her body, unused to any physical exertion more strenuous than that of the ballroom, ached in every limb and in every muscle. Her feet, which had originally been clad in soft kid slippers tied with satin ribbons, now slithered in a tangled morass of torn stockings and bleeding blisters.

Sighing deeply, she took the sensible decision that she would not think of the Earl, left behind in such uncomfortable and dangerous conditions, just as she would not think of the number of miles she might yet have to walk. The decision, while easy to take, was remarkably difficult to act upon, and she had not travelled more than two hundred yards through the woods before she found herself counting every step taken by her burning feet, and quivering at every snap of a twig for fear that it might be a pistol shot marking the end of the Earl's existence.

Once clear of the small wood, she found herself at the outskirts of the Home Farm pastures, and in the bright light of early morning she abandoned any attempt to conceal her presence. There seemed almost no possibility that the *Baron's* servants would run the risk of pursuing her here, and with luck she might encounter one of the milkmaids, or even one of the farm labourers setting off for a day's ditch-digging.

She found that the increasing warmth of the sun left her strangely light-headed, while her body—lacking the protection of a cloak since the day before—seemed alternately burning hot and freezing cold. She felt as though she had already walked for miles, although one part of her brain did remember that she had not crossed more than two large fields. When first she saw the group of figures clustered on the horizon she fought back the surge of hope that filled her being, telling herself that the stolid figures could not be anything more than the figments of her own disordered imagination.

But the comforting group of bodies remained outlined

against the horizon, moving slowly in her direction. With a moan of relief, she picked up the tattered remnants of her once-elegant afternoon gown, and forced the leaden lumps that had once been her feet into the semblance of a run. The glad cries of recognition sprang out to greet her when she was still separated from her rescuers by fifty yards of muddy grass. One tiny figure thrust itself in front of the group and ran down the sloping pasture to meet her.

"Oh ma'am, your ladyship. Oh ma'am. Your ladyship's shoes! You'm hurt bad, my lady!" Annie stood awkwardly, and rubbed both her hands against the heavy worsted of her cape. "You can be leaning on me, my lady, if you likes. Mr. Smith and some of the lads will be with us directly."

Thankfully Marianne abandoned the pretence of self-sufficiency. Smith, startled out of his habitual stolidity, puffed up to them, and she felt her body sway against his wiry frame. "The Earl . . . is imprisoned in the chapel . . ." she gasped. "Take care. There are men outside, and one has a musket."

She stared with a vague sense of irritation at the circle of horrified and immobile servants who surrounded her. Since she had given no thought to the ashen pallor of her face, nor to the blood that liberally bedaubed the remains of her clothing, she could not understand their shocked expressions. She knew only that a thick cloud was coming down, separating her from her rescuers, but she tried once again to penetrate the mist. "The Earl . . ." she said. "Wounded . You must hurry."

The brief commands had exhausted her. She had no more strength left for the herculean task of remaining on her feet, so with a small sigh she collapsed into an untidy heap in the middle of her astonished servants.

CHAPTER SEVENTEEN

Marianne sat quietly on the boudoir chair, and allowed Becky to scold her as she wound her mistress's long hair into a soft coil of curls dressed modishly on the crown of her head. Marianne waited until the last pin was in place and then said firmly, "You may as well hold your breath, Becky, for I have already decided that today I am going to leave my bedchamber."

"And what about your poor feet, my lady. Have you thought about them?"

"I can *assure* you, Becky, that there are few things I have thought about more frequently during the past three days. But I shall wear my silk slippers that we brought home from India. They will not rub against the bandages."

Becky sniffed disapprovingly. "Miss Thatcher spent all day yesterday in here gossiping, not to mention that nice Mr. Packenham. And Sir Henry Lane came up only this morning to tell you all the latest news. Why do you have to go gallivanting around the house? His lordship's surgeon —*not* that I think he can be compared to our Mr. Green who has always given you such excellent service in the past —won't promise even now that you have avoided a congestion of the lungs."

"Becky, I am clearly not suffering from so much as a

light chill, let alone lung disease. And since the Earl is unable to leave his rooms, I wish to see for myself how his wound is healing."

Becky was silent, being unable with propriety to voice any opposition to such a statement, and yet still concerned that her mistress would succumb to miscellaneous unspecified sicknesses if once allowed to leave the sanctuary of her bedchamber. She took refuge in a change of conversation, while she fussed around various drawers looking for a warm spencer and a woolly shawl.

"What did Sir Henry say about those heathen foreigners that tried to run off with you?" she asked. "Smith told me that the *Conte* was certain to die."

"The *Conte* di Mazaretto had a concussion, but both he and the *Baron* are now recovering. Our government does not plan to imprison them, but will send them back to Italy as soon as they are fit to travel. From what Sir Henry tells me concerning Prince Alberto's methods of punishing his enemies, I think they might have preferred to stay in England, but our government wished to avoid the outcry that would be caused by a public trial."

"Well, my lady, they're only going to get the treatment they deserve," said Becky, who saw no reason to hesitate in meting out the sort of vigorous justice generally advocated in her favourite Old Testament. "And I understand that the Dowager Countess and Lady Eleanor will be moving into the Dower House very shortly," she added slyly. "I don't suppose you'll be complaining about that."

"The Earl's mother and sister must always be welcome in my house," said Marianne virtuously and with a complete lack of truth. "But I believe the Dowager would prefer to have an independent household."

Becky sniffed meaningfully, but said grudgingly, "If you insist on going visiting, my lady, I suppose you are ready now."

She wrapped a shawl around her mistress's shoulders, ignoring Marianne's complaint that she now resembled a bundle of linen parcelled up for the washerwoman. In truth, when once outside her door, Marianne found the corridors very chilly, and her legs still considerably more shaky than she liked to admit, even to herself.

Smith answered her timid knock on the Earl's door, and led her with formal bows of approval into the most comfortable chair in the Earl's sitting room.

"If you would be so good as to wait for one or two minutes, my lady, I will apprise his lordship of your ladyship's arrival. We are much improved in health and spirits today, my lady, and will no doubt be pleased to welcome you. May I say, my lady, how gratified I am to see your ladyship once more restored to health?"

"That is very good of you," said Marianne deducing from the flow of elevated formalities that she had been successful in gaining admission to the circle of people blessed with Smith's approval. "I am pleased the Earl is feeling better," she added.

The one or two minutes had stretched out considerably before Marianne heard the sound of footsteps entering the sitting-room. She turned round quickly and saw that her husband had entered the room alone. Suddenly shy, and all too conscious of the great difference between this formal meeting and their last dangerous moments together, she lowered her eyes and examined the fringes of her shawl with every appearance of total fascination.

The Earl broke the absurdly lengthening silence. "You must forgive the unconventional nature of my attire," he said. "I am afraid that even Smith's best efforts could not coax any of my coats over the remaining wad of bandages. I trust you do not find my dressing-gown offensive."

"Oh no, no. Not at all," said Marianne, nearly distracted by the cold courtesy of his tones. "I am delighted to see that your recovery is proceeding so well."

"And what of yourself?" enquired the Earl politely. "The surgeon assured me that you had suffered no lasting damage and my uncle told me that you were full of energetic questions when he visited you."

"Oh I am very well, thank you," said Marianne miserably. "Except for a few dozen bruises and blisters you might say that I am as good as new."

With four or five swift strides, the Earl was by her side, kneeling down beside her and taking both her hands in his own firm clasp. "Ah Marianne," he said with a hint of laughter in his voice. "If I am very humble and beg your pardon for my appalling behaviour when we first met, and for my outrageous conduct in dragging you into one of my uncle's eternal political escapades, do you think you might see a way to forgive me? I fear my weakened constitution cannot endure many more minutes of such strained courtesy between us. I confess that I have become attached to a rather less dutiful wife."

Marianne tried to look offended. "Pupils of Miss Beale's Academy for the Daughters of Gentlemen are *always* noted for their courtesy, and for their sense of duty, my lord."

The Earl pulled her to her feet with a ruthless show of

strength. "Then I shall put Miss Beale's instruction to the test by commanding you to remain still whilst I kiss you."

Marianne obligingly demonstrated the superiority of Miss Beale's methods of teaching by remaining quite still while the Earl placed his hand firmly beneath her chin and raised her lips to receive his kiss. After a considerable elapse of time she rested her head upon the lapel of his dressing-gown and spoke into the folds of his shirt.

"I am so relieved that the *Conte* did not succeed in killing you," she said. She ventured a quick look at his face. "Was the *Conte*'s sister very beautiful?" she asked in a small voice.

The Earl looked momentarily confused. "I might have known that you would seize upon the one part of di Mazaretto's conversation that any gentlewoman would have striven to forget," he said resignedly.

"But I am not a gentlewoman," said Marianne with considerable triumph. "I used to be a tradesman's daughter, and *now* I am a Countess, which is an altogether superior state of affairs to being a mere gentlewoman."

"You are a baggage," said the Earl severely. He cupped Marianne's face between his hands and dropped a fleeting kiss on the softness of her lips. "Yes," he said. "The *Principessa* was very beautiful." He waited for Marianne's lashes to close over the deep violet of her eyes, before whispering softly, "But from what I have seen so far, nowhere near as beautiful as you."

Marianne's eyes flew open in astonishment and a light blush coloured her cheeks. Laughingly, the Earl drew her close, stilling her half-hearted protest with his kiss. "I can see that with such an inquisitive wife I shall be obliged to lay down the strictest rules for your behaviour." His fingers traced the delicate curve of her cheek. "The first and most important of these rules is that you shall always love me as much as I love you. And the second of these. . . ." He paused for a moment and looked down searchingly at his wife.

"Yes," she said softly. "And what is the second rule?"

"The second rule can wait until later," said the Earl. "Just now I have better things to do." His arms crushed Marianne to him in a long and tempestuous embrace.

"Quentin!" Marianne protested. "Remember your wound!"

The Earl laughed quietly. "The second rule," he said, "is never to interrupt your husband when he is engaged in making passionate love to his wife."

Marianne moved more closely into his arms. "In this, as in all things, my lord, I shall strive to be an obedient wife."

Masquerade
Historical Romances

Intrigue excitement romance

Don't miss
October's
other enthralling Historical Romance title

ZULU SUNSET
by Christina Laffeaty

When Cassandra Hudson inherits a fortune, it seems the ideal opportunity to remind her cousin Martin — whom she has always loved — that she might be a desirable missionary's wife. How can he reject a girl who travels all the way to remote Zululand for his sake, and who is willing to give her inheritance to his Magwana Mission?

Unfortunately the year is 1879, and Zululand is in dangerous ferment. Cassandra cannot even reach Martin — except with the help of Saul Parnell, an arrogant Englishman brought up by natives to become a white Zulu chief, appointed by King Cetewayo. And why should he bother with Cassandra's problems when he is facing the impending war between whites and Zulus?

You can obtain this title today from your local paperback retailer